C000170445

Ms Kellet has written a fast paced book that will delight fans of lurid village life. The characters are believable – one can visualise them walking down any village street in England and the suspects are the ordinary people of everyday life. On the surface that is, beneath that smooth everyday exterior lurk individual minds that remind us of our own personal contradictions and complications. A compelling book with a satisfying resolution.

– Peter Dicken

First published in Great Britain as a softback original in 2021

Copyright © Glenis Kellet

The moral right of this author has been asserted.

Typeset in ITC Galliard Pro

Editing, design, typesetting and publishing by UK Book Publishing

www.ukbookpublishing.com

ISBN: 978-1-914195-55-6

LETHAL REVENGE

Glenis Kellet

LETHAL REVENGE

Lethal Revenge

THUD!

The horrendous sound of a victim's fragile head, crashing down onto a dense, sandstone slab in the greenhouse. The victim had been knocked to the floor with a terrific blow; blood oozed out of a fatal gash to the back of her head. The blood slowly pooled and congealed around her short, curly grey hair.

The perpetrator quickly dropped the heavy blood-splattered object from his gloved hand. His bare arms, face, and T-shirt marked him as a killer with the bright red splatter of innocent blood. He dashed to the house and tried the door handle to the backdoor; he was in luck – his victim had left it unlocked!

Leaving blood smears on the door handle, he ran around the house leaving a trail of smears; he was searching for anything of value. He rifled through a leather wallet, looking for any money he could find. He gleefully took

£50 in notes and a few coins he had found on top of the tallboy in the main bedroom. He hurriedly stuffed them into his jeans pocket and ran to the back door; he hastily sprinted down the long garden path – glancing towards the open door of the long greenhouse, to the body lying motionless inside. His lips curled in a sinful smile at the sight of his heinous crime. He fled through the back gate; his heart was pounding furiously, adrenalin was surging through him, giving him an ultra 'high'. He raced to his parked car and sped off.

The following day, Flora – an elderly friend of the murdered victim – arrived for tea. She knocked on the front door but there was no reply; she knocked several times. She attempted to turn the door handle – it was locked. Flora had her own key to the house, so she was able to let herself in. *Perhaps my friend is in the bathroom,* Flora thought to herself.

"Amy, Amy are you there, love?" she shouted, walking towards the backroom; she could smell the aroma of homemade bread. There was no reply, only stillness and the eerie sound of a ticking clock situated on the mantelpiece. The elderly woman wandered around the house searching every room, calling her friend's name, and wondering if Amy had forgotten she was coming that day.

When Flora saw the blood smears everywhere she naively wondered if her friend had cut her hand – she was always having accidents in the garden and cutting herself in the kitchen. She looked out of the spare bedroom window to see if Amy had driven off in her car – to the hospital perhaps? – to have her wound attended to. But Flora saw her car was still parked, in its usual place at the dead end in the back lane.

Flora then thought her friend may be outside gardening, although she hadn't seen her there through the spare bedroom window. Confused at not finding Amy ready to greet her, she slipped out of the unlocked back door to have a look. No, she didn't appear to be in the garden; she was half expecting Amy to walk up behind her or appear from behind a bush holding her secateurs.

Suddenly, a high-pitched scream rang through the quiet garden – Flora had found her friend's lifeless body in the greenhouse! Amy's head was lying in a pool of blood. The birds took flight at the piercing noise, flapping their wings and soaring into the bright blue sky. Wide eyed with horror, the elderly woman fled from the greenhouse back into the garden. In that split second Flora was deciding what to do; she was afraid the killer was still lurking around the property. She ran panic stricken to the back gate, fearing to enter the blood smeared house again, and ran as fast as she could to the front of the house. Her heart was racing so fast and so loud in her chest, she thought it would burst. She jumped into her car and drove away at full speed. She pulled into a lay-by and rang the police on her mobile phone; her words tumbled off her tongue in an erratic and panicky way.

"Amy – she's dead! ... Come quickly... she's just...

lying there!" Flora puffed – the shock had affected her breathing and she was hyperventilating.

The policewoman who had taken the phone call, had to gently calm the elderly lady down to make sense of what had happened. Slowly the information required to locate the body was gently drawn out of the panicked, hysterical woman. The policewoman had also concluded that it was a possible homicide with the description she had received regarding the blood splattered object lying near the body.

Several police cars arrived with armed police officers in a van; an ambulance arrived on the scene shortly after. Immediately the back garden was searched for the killer or killers; they pronounced the garden secure and moved on into the house. The medics pronounced Amy dead at the scene and the crime scene investigators began their meticulous investigation of processing the crime scene.

Amy was a widow in her late 60s. The deadly weapon used lay at the scene by her side, as described by the dead woman's friend, splattered with blood. It was a heavy brass door stopper used to stop the greenhouse door from slamming shut.

There were two detectives there on the scene – the older colleague, Detective Chief Inspector Alex Crawford, and his junior, Detective Inspector Sam Johnson. Both were good friends in and out of work. They made a phenomenal team together.

"The victim may have known her killer – Amy had obviously turned away from her attacker to be struck from behind, or the killer had crept up behind her and hit her violently on the back of her head; without her hearing him," observed DI Johnson, speaking out his thoughts aloud.

DCI Crawford, perceiving the situation closely, replied "She would have seen anyone approaching from here unless she was preoccupied with something else. The greenhouse stands in the middle of the garden, she had a 360-degree view of the surroundings. The killer didn't appear to have arrived with a weapon, look..." He pointed to the brass door stopper on the floor by the body. "The perpetrator took the nearest thing to hand to kill her."

The wooden greenhouse was painted white, it was quite long with doors at either end. Amy was lying near to the door closest to the garden path.

Amy was small in height and slightly overweight, her green cotton summer dress fitting tightly to her upper torso. The light brown sandals she was wearing were askew on her bare feet. A slug trail glistened in the sunshine leading to the pool of blood. Flies were already buzzing around and landing on the corpse's blood-soaked matted hair; crawling into the deep bloodied open wound in the back of her head. The plants in the greenhouse appeared to be bowing their heads in sympathy – they were dehydrated from the heat and lack of water. These vertical plants were tied to their canes – tomatoes, cucumbers, and sweet peppers; they wouldn't have been watered for a while.

"It looks like she died yesterday, in the afternoon, I'll confirm a clearer time after I've performed the post-mortem back at the mortuary," the forensic pathologist announced as he struggled to stand up after examining her lifeless body. He mopped his sweaty brow with a white handkerchief and sighed.

Deep in thought, the two detectives surveyed the garden; it was mainly a fruit and vegetable garden with an orchard – hens were clucking and pecking in the grass, behind a tall chicken wired fence; unaware of what was going on. The onions in long rows had their tops folded over; potato leaves were beginning to yellow at the far end of the plot. There were several neat plots all growing different types of vegetables. Pots stood on the patio area with different varieties of lettuce growing in them. Blueberries were beginning to ripen on several bushes. There were juicy strawberries galore, ripe, and ready to be picked. In the orchard, apples and pears trees were laden with unripened fruit.

The two detectives walked solemnly down the stone flagged pathway; they could hear the constant rumbling sound coming from the distant motorway to the east. A small bumblebee was busy collecting the abundance of nectar from a blackberry bush, it had alighted on one of the pinkish coloured petals making up the dainty flower, amongst a cluster of other flowers. DCI Crawford glanced at the wonderful display nature was providing him, *the beauty of Mother Nature carries on regardless of what the human world creates for itself* – he pondered quietly to himself. A long branch from the bush had been staked in a vertical position yet had continued to grow and was arching over the washing line. A few white bath towels were pegged on the line.

The house had been pronounced as being secure by the police firearms team; they left once their job had been completed. The two detectives strolled on towards the small white painted house; they stepped over the threshold of the doorway, in white shoe covers and disposable plastic gloves they had put on at the doorstep in order to protect the crime scene.

In the kitchen, the smell of newly baked bread drew their eyes to half a dozen white bread rolls that had cooled on a wire tray. The sink was full of dirty dishes and pans; on the white tiled kitchen windowsill, there were a few dead black flies beside a fly swatter. Paint pots, paintbrushes, a wooden stirrer, and paint rags were placed on a cardboard sheet on the unit top.

"Amy appeared to be a handy sort of woman by the looks of things, doing her own maintenance," DCI Crawford mentioned, thinking out aloud. He thought it was such a waste of a human life. A latched wooden door was open, leading into a walk-in pantry. Strange looking things in jars immediately grabbed their attention.

"Looks like she stored things the old fashioned way," the DCI commented. Bottles and jars stood in rows on the wooden shelves. A few were labelled 'cider vinegar' – they had apple cores floating on top of a clear liquid inside the jars. Another large jar was labelled 'orange peel'. There were jars of string beans in salt, beetroot in vinegar, and jars of different types of jams and jellies. Dried peas and beans stood in a few tall glass jars; a large round storage jar was full of pickled eggs, on the shelf above. The DI lifted a lid on a large glazed pot that stood on the stone flagged floor.

"Ugh, salted cabbage I think," he remarked, rather amused. At the end of the room stood an upturned wooden stool, with a muslin cloth tied to the four legs. Laid on the cloth was a red mushy lump of stewed fruit; the red juice was percolating through the muslin cloth and was slowly dripping into a glass bowl beneath – reminding them of the blooded scene outside.

Onions were strung up on hooks from the ceiling with bunches of wilted herbs cascading down from other hooks giving off a strange mixed aroma. A tray laid on the floor was full of what appeared to be crushed eggshells.

DI Johnson chuckled. "It's like going back in time in here, a completely different way of life and there's no deep freeze!" They walked back into the old fashioned kitchen – all the units were free-standing. An old cooker was wedged between them; it had an eye-level grill. The large white ceramic sink had a set of old fashioned taps stood tall over the sink. There was a small fridge stood on one of the unit tops; it was humming quietly.

The rest of the house was thoroughly searched; blood smears were all over the house – on the walls, the banister rail, doorknob, and drawer handles. In the main bedroom, the victim's bed was still unmade, clothes hung up on hangers hung from the top of a wardrobe. Her pink summer nightie was strewn over her crumpled duvet.

"This wallet has been tampered with, there are blood smears inside and no money in it," the DI stated as he observed the empty wallet on top of the tallboy.

"It could've been an opportunist wanting cash but it doesn't explain why he or she had to kill Amy!" exclaimed the other detective. They searched another bedroom; it was small with a single bed, made up, with a double wardrobe and empty shelving in an alcove.

They walked into a box room which had been made into an office – papers and files were everywhere. Lots of photographs mounted in frames hung around the walls. Many were of Amy's late husband they assumed, near a lake and a wood.

There were photographs of deer quietly grazing near the fringes of the wood and magnificent close-up shots of dragonflies. There were a few fantastic shots of swifts swooping in for insects near the surface of the calm water in the lake. Striking phenomenal pictures of carp jumping out of the lake and diving back in caught their eye – it was a clever trick to remove parasites. It was a spectacular record of their acrobatic antics in the stunning sunsets. DI Johnson, being an angler, had seen the display in real life, many times.

A computer sat on an old shabby desk with a printer and keyboard. The DI opened a cupboard; it was full of box files. He pulled one out; it was labelled 'Dating men'. He examined the contents.

"This looks interesting! ... She looks as if she was on a dating site and had recorded each potential suitor's details, email address, and telephone number. You wouldn't think a woman her age would be interested in finding a partner!"

"Perhaps she was lonely and wanted a partner for companionship," DCI Crawford suggested.

"Oh, look here! she records – 'Len Cartwright – he's definitely looking for a mummy wife and it ain't gonna be me!'" DI Johnson smiled. "She's got a sense of humour! ... 'Adrian Jackson', she writes; 'he's just after my money!' – Perhaps one of these men could be her killer! Look, another, 'Ben Walton – he's as bald as a coot – a total sex maniac!' she wrote." They both gave out a little laugh.

"We'll take these with us, check if there is anything else of interest," DCI Crawford advised.

They were 'melting' in the humid heatwave as they searched the untidy office. Their shirts were sticking to their sweaty torsos and perspiration ran down from their brows.

"There's a file on a court case here with a man we know well – Stuart Wilson, we know him as a bit of a con man – looks like her case against him was thrown out on technicalities. She's nicknamed him 'half digit'."

"It wasn't long ago, our chaps were called to his house for a case of domestic abuse, it was reported by his neighbours; he was allegedly accused, by his wife, of hitting her. He could be our man!"

The DCI picked up another box file labelled 'Lodgers'; he quickly read the contents. "She's had dozens of lodgers over the years, any one of these could be her killer."

Suddenly, Amy's telephone rang making the detectives jump. DCI Crawford lifted the receiver.

"Hello Amy darling, how is your day going?" an amorous male's voice asked.

"Who is speaking please?" asked the DCI – the phone suddenly went dead. The detectives continued their search. "I'll have this computer examined; I'll get one of the lads to take it back to the office; there may be some vital clues in it," the DCI suggested.

"Hey, look here! Amy's will, a solicitor's firm in the town are the executors, I'll give them a ring so they can set the ball rolling," remarked DI Johnson.

"Who are the beneficiaries?" quizzed the curious DCI.

The pages were turned and swiftly read. "Paul White inherits the property and Florence Clarke will receive anything left after expenses," came the reply.

The DCI's mobile phone interrupted their conversation, toning a melody tune.

A serious voice began to speak at the other end – "We have another murder; the body was found at 'The Eaves' pub in Blackendale."

"We're on our way," answered the astonished DCI, finishing the call. He turned to his colleague. "We'll go to the Blackendale Pub, there's been another murder; we'll take these box files and other files with us to sort through later. We will also have to interview the woman who found Amy. Perhaps she could enlighten us about the murdered victim's background and if she has relatives we need to contact. The woman should have calmed down by then and be ready to talk."

Removing their protective coverings, the two concerned detectives left, leaving the hive of activity in the house. The team of forensics continued with their work of trying to find fingerprints and any DNA of Amy's killer or killers. The detectives saw the black body bag, containing Amy's body, being lifted into a vehicle as they hurried down the back garden path to their car on the grass verge; the car was parked outside the yellow barrier tape which was cordoning off the crime scene. They saw police officers further down the lane as they drove away; they were knocking on doors to question the neighbours; they were asking if they had seen or heard anything suspicious the day before when the murder had taken place.

The detectives travelled the six miles to 'The Eaves' pub in Blackendale. A rumble of thunder could be heard in the distance and several moments later a flash of lightning streaked through the darkening sky.

There was a commotion outside the tiny stone-built country pub; villagers had gathered around the main door, curious as to what had gone on. Police were moving them back and reeling out the crime scene tape to cordon off the area. It would prevent the curious crowd from looking through the windows at the investigation of the crime scene.

The two detectives were allowed through into the cordoned area of the car park and entered by the little wooden back door of the pub, wearing their protective clothing. The powerful, malty aromas of beer met their nostrils; it increased in intensity as they walked into the main room.

A police officer filled them in on a few details. "Her brother found her about an hour ago, she's Jane Hughes, 66 years old, she's the landlady here. The pub has been closed due to the sale and purchase. She was checking things before handing over the keys today. A woman across the road recalls hearing footsteps running away from the pub from her opened bedroom window, at about six this morning."

"Nick, the pathologist will be here soon; he has had a busy afternoon – there was another murder at Raystone!" the senior detective informed the police officer.

"Same M.O. here, look! The victim was struck on the back of the head with that empty bottle," observed DI Johnson. The bottle lay shattered on the carpet, dried blood could clearly be seen on some of the pieces and shards of glass.

The portly forensic pathologist rushed in. "Not another! Two murders in one day, it's a record for me!" He knelt down; he was breathing heavily and sweating profusely. "Switch on all the lights, will you, I can't see a damn thing in here!" he ordered.

He observed the mottling of the skin on her arms and legs as her blood had pooled after death. "Initial estimate of the time of death – I'd say earlier this morning. She's been bludgeoned to death by blows to the back of the head with this bottle, I would think. I'll tell you more when I've finished examining the body at the mortuary." He struggled to stand up with his overweight physique, he adjusted his red framed glasses and stared around the room.

DCI Crawford had walked around the bar; he saw the till was closed. He opened the old fashioned cash drawer with his handkerchief – it was empty. The money could have been removed by the landlady before the keys were to be handed over, he figured. He observed a row of old keys, on the top of the bar; each with a hand written label tied to them with string – ready for the takeover. He had already noticed the key in the back door and saw there was another spare key labelled 'back door', lying on top of the bar.

The whole building was searched from top to bottom by the forensic team who had arrived shortly after Nick, the forensic pathologist. It was a quaint, little old English public house. The sign outside hung on a wrought iron wall bracket high up on the stone wall over the oak front door of the pub. It had large black letters spelling the words 'The Eaves'.

Inside the cosy little pub were oak beamed ceilings which were quite low; the windows were small, draped with little red curtains. Wooden tables and chairs were arranged around the dimly lit room. A wood burning stove sat in an inglenook fireplace at the far end, horse brasses hung from the stonework. A large TV screen was mounted on the wall. In front of the small bar was a line of wooden bar stools.

There were a few tiny rooms in the pub, all had a serving hatch linking to the bar. There was only one toilet for the males and one for the female visitors; both were searched. Upstairs was a small empty flat and a storeroom.

Downstairs, stone steps led down to the cellar, from a back room. The cellar was the full length of the building containing the metal kegs of alcoholic beverages that would quench the thirst of the villagers. Outside was a row of stone garages converted from old stables – logs were heaped in one corner in the end garage. There was nothing found out of place in the little country pub – the body was the only evidence of an audacious loathsome crime.

"We'll interview her brother in the office," DCI Crawford instructed.

A short, potbellied man walked into the neat office at the back of the pub; he looked bewildered and distressed.

"Come and take a seat, we need to ask you a few questions," stated the DCI. The thunder outside rumbled on in sudden intermittent intervals throughout the interview.

Later in the conversation, the detective asked if there had been anything stolen.

"No, we had already moved out, we had cleared out the till and the charity boxes out of the pub yesterday." The man thought for a moment. "My sister Jane always had a handbag with her in case she needed her asthma medication. I didn't see the bag when I found her. Did you?"

"No, we didn't see a bag. Did she generally keep cash in her handbag or did she only use credit cards?" queried the detective.

"She used both," came the reply.

"What kind of handbag did she have?" he was asked.

"I think it would be her light brown shoulder bag today as she is wearing her fawn-coloured skirt and jacket."

A police officer rushed into the office. "Sir, I've found a handbag in the skip outside under a load of rubbish." He placed the light brown shoulder bag on the office desk with his plastic gloved hand.

"Is this your sister's handbag?" the DCI asked.

"Yes! It is," the deceased woman's brother declared.

The detective looked inside. "There's no purse, only a set of keys, her asthma inhaler, a packet of paper hankies and a plastic wallet containing a credit card and a debit card. Bag this up for forensics, will you, there may be prints on it." He handed it back to the young police officer. "You have done well!"

The young police officer smiled; he was pleased with himself for finding vital evidence. He jauntily walked out of the office holding the evidence.

After the lengthy interview with the deceased's brother, the detectives discussed the case.

"Same M.O. and possibly cash stolen with her purse –

we may have a serial killer on our hands!" DCI Crawford grimly announced.

"I don't ever remember having a serial killer in this area before!" exclaimed his junior detective, his eyes shining with enthusiasm for the case.

"I think the last one was early last century! Long before my time," his older colleague replied.

Earlier that morning, a young local boy had been out riding his bike on the quiet road by the church near to his house. A flash of red in the grass was noticed in the corner of his eye; he stopped. He quickly jumped off his bike, he was eager to bend down and see what the bright red object laid on the grass verge could be. He was delighted, thinking it was an injured bird of some sort, that he could care for. To his disappointment, it was just an old red clasp purse laid open in the grass. He picked it up and took it home.

He forgot about it until teatime when his mum and dad were talking about the pub murder; he ran to fetch the purse.

"Look what I've found, can I keep it, Mum?" he asked, wide eyed in anticipation.

"Let me look..." His mother scrutinized the purse, then it dawned on her – "Oh no, it may belong to Jane Hughes from the pub. I'll take it to the police. Where did you find it?"

"Down by the church, I was riding my bike down there this morning, it was in the grass! I thought it was a red bird at first. Please can I keep it, I found it!" the young boy pleaded.

His mum tried to explain about the murder and that the purse could possibly be evidence for the police. She explained to him about fingerprints so he could understand. The boy was quite excited to think he may have found vital evidence to solve a real live murder!

"Now stay indoors until the bad man is found, I don't want you being murdered."

The boy wasn't afraid at all, it was all tremendously thrilling to him. He excitedly ran upstairs to play cops and baddies with his teddy!

The sky looked threatening as the storm was rolling closer. The police were going door to door; they were asking everyone for information about the person running from the scene or any other information they could tell them about.

"Did you see a parked vehicle or bike or a person near the pub at about six this morning," the policewoman politely asked the milkman. He was lifting crates of milk bottles from his pickup and carrying them to his cold room in his garage. He was stacking the last crate when the policewoman and her colleague entered his yard. He walked out of the cold room and shut the door.

He scratched his head in deep thought. "Aye, I did, come to think about it. I didn't really take much notice, but I can tell you it was a blue estate car of some sort. It was parked up by that wall there." He pointed to a tall stone garden wall about 100 metres from the pub.

"Did you see anyone in the vehicle or the registration number?" the policewoman asked.

"As far as I remember it was empty. No, I didn't look at the number plate," the milkman replied.

The area was searched along the tall stone wall, but unfortunately, there was no evidence found.

The elderly woman across the road from the pub was questioned. "You have reported you heard a person running from the pub at about six this morning; did you notice anything else?" a police officer asked.

"Well now, let me think for a minute – I did wake up before then, it must have been when Jane was turning her car into the pub car park. I never heard anything else until the running sound at about six."

The policewoman knocked on another door with her colleague stood beside her, they could hear a dog furiously barking behind the closed door. The door opened slightly and a man's gaunt, unshaven face appeared through the gap. A dog's black nose was trying desperately to squeeze through the opening in the doorway; questions were asked from the police officers.

"My dog started barking around six. I told him to shut up and go back to sleep!" exclaimed the young male, breathing out stale cigarette smoke from his mouth. The officers walked away after thanking him.

"No joy there then," the policewoman moaned as they continued their door-to-door inquiry.

The two detectives in the pub were still discussing the case.

"We'll have to find out if these two murders are linked apart from them having a similar M.O.," the DCI announced. They returned to their car to drive to Amy's friend's house to ask her some questions about Amy.

As they passed the village bus stop, they observed a woman disembarking from the last bus; her teenage daughter had hurried to meet her.

"Have you heard about the murder in the pub?" the chubby girl with pigtails excitedly asked. She was taking one of the plastic carrier bags from her mother's hand as she spoke.

"Gosh no, who's been murdered?" her mother asked anxiously, raising her hand to her mouth in shock.

"It's Jane Hughes! Murdered early this morning, her brother found her this afternoon," the chubby girl declared.

"Oh no, poor woman, and she's just sold the pub and going to start a new life." She looked across at the pub as they walked down the road. The forensic investigation team was packing up their vehicles, she could see Jane's brother walking around the car park perplexed and confused. "Poor man, he will miss her. I heard there has been another murder in Raystone but I don't know her; I think it was Amy Lewis or some name like that. She was murdered in her own greenhouse!"

"She's the woman that owned the fishing lake and the woods, don't you remember!" her daughter exclaimed.

"Oh yes, of course, I do, now I think of it. Perhaps there's a serial killer on the loose, we've never had a murder around these parts before. We'll all be too afraid to go into our gardens now and are we safe in our own houses?"

"We'll have to stick together from now on, we don't want to be his third victim!"

Flora's Information

The detectives arrived in the nearby town and located Amy's friend's address – Flora had given her own address when she had rung the police after finding Amy's body.

There stood a block of six flats in front of them. The detective chief inspector pressed a button on the intercom labelled 'Flora', it was situated outside, in the doorway – a female's raspy voice responded with "Hello".

"It's the police, could we talk to you about your friend Amy?"

"Yes, of course, come on up, I've been expecting you," the raspy voice replied.

The door buzzed, the detective opened it and they both ascended the worn out carpeted stairs to the second floor.

"Please come in," the woman beckoned. "I'm feeling less shaky after the dreadful shock of finding my poor, dear friend. I'm Florence Clarke but call me Flora. Amy was the only one who called me Flo, you know." She led them into her neat comfortable lounge. The window was open allowing a breeze to flow around the room. There was a loud clap of thunder and seconds later a violent streak of lightning, lighting up the dark menacing sky – the storm was moving closer.

"Take a seat," Flora suggested. She was a frail looking woman in her late 70s, her hair was tied back in a tight bun. Wisps of grey hair fell onto the collar of her short sleeved, floral cotton dress. The skin on her thin arms was wrinkled with age. She adjusted her pink bifocals on her thin, bony nose and stared at the detectives.

"We would like you to tell us how you found Amy," asked the senior detective, sitting down on the sofa with his colleague.

Flora informed them of the horrendous experience, the best she could through her emotional tears. Rain began to patter against the window, Flora struggled out of her armchair and walked over to close the top window. There was a sudden downpour, rain lashed angrily against the glass.

"What is Amy's full name, does she have any close relatives who should be informed?" DCI Crawford inquired.

"Her full name is Amy Catherine Lewis, she doesn't have any relatives – no children; I'm the only close person in her life, apart from a lodger she once had. She treated him like a son; probably because she didn't have any of her own. He left last year to go and live with his girlfriend but he's often around to see Amy, they had a special bond between them just like mother and son; he will be devastated when he hears the dreadful news."

"What is his name and where does he live?" asked the lead detective.

"Oh dear, I'm not very good at remembering names, let me think now… Paul, yes, I think he's called Paul, he lives in the town somewhere."

"We'll probably find his name in the lodger's file," the DI thought out aloud. He had remembered a Paul being the main beneficiary to Amy's will.

"Yes, she was very meticulous about recording everything as her memory wasn't brilliant either!" replied Flora. She continued – "Paul is a nice young man, had a tragic past I believe, he lost both his parents at a young age and was brought up by his Auntie and Uncle. He's a thoughtful person too, he used to offer to do Amy's shopping at the supermarket on his way home from work. He used to take her out for meals – mind you, I think Amy insisted on paying."

"We have found her will and we have notified her executors," DCI Crawford informed Flora.

"Yes, I know all about her will, I have a copy here. Amy and I discussed it a few times, we always thought I would die first as I'm a lot older than Amy. She's willed the property to Paul, the young man who was like a son to her. Well, she had no one else and wanted to make sure he had a property of his own; that's how close they were. She never told him he was going to inherit her property. She left me a little bit too in case I outlived her or if I wasn't around it would go to a charity."

"I see, I'm glad she didn't let Paul know about the will or he would be our number one suspect," remarked the DI.

"No, he definitely never knew anything about her will," Flora emphatically declared.

"What about the men in Amy's life?" DCI Crawford quizzed. His voice faded into the distance as Flora's thoughts strayed to happier times with her friend Amy.

"Are you hearing me?" the DCI asked; he could see Flora drift off into a world of her own.

Her body jolted. "Pardon, what did you say?" Her misty eyes came out of the glazed look and centred on the detective.

"What about the men in Amy's life?" he repeated, raising his voice.

"Oh," Flora continued, "her husband died a while back, they owned the woods and the lake adjoining the property, they used to have anglers fishing the lake and had walks and picnic areas in the woods for the paying public. It was a beautiful, idyllic place. When her husband died Amy sold that off and kept the house and plot of land."

"Did she have any trouble with anglers or the public using the lake and the wooded area?" Flora was asked.

"Yes, she did! She banned a few for not paying or constantly breaking the rules. She had her tyres slashed once, probably for revenge – she reported it to the police, but nothing ever came of it." Flora dried a tear from her eye with her long thin bony finger. "Amy had an electric gate installed; to stop people driving their cars into the property who didn't have a coded magnetic key to open the gate. Anglers had to become members and buy a coded key. The woods, well they were closed down for the general public. Such a shame, it's only a small percentage that spoils it for everyone, every time!"

"Did she date other men?" the DCI queried.

"Oh yes, I think Paul put her up to that! Amy had told him she was lonely. She joined one of these dating sites on her computer, I tried to persuade her not to, you never know who will do you harm!" Flora sighed. "Mind you, Amy told me – 'from what I can see, the best men are married, I'm left with men seeking money, sex or a mummy wife!'" Flora chuckled, she could still hear those words spoken by Amy, even now.

"Were there any particular men that she didn't like or was afraid of?" Flora was asked.

"I don't know about that but there was one man absolutely obsessed with her! Amy politely told him where to go! He still phoned her up occasionally, I think he's just lonely."

The detectives remembered the phone call in Amy's office that had made both of them jump – maybe it was him, trying to phone Amy.

"What was his name and where does he live?" DCI Crawford questioned.

"I've no idea, she just used to call him, 'the idiot'!" Flora chuckled.

The detectives smiled. "Has Amy had a court case against anyone?" Flora was asked.

"Ooh yes, come to think about it; she took the vending machine man to court, this was when her husband was alive and they sold drinks and snacks from the vending machines, in a hut near the woods. The court case never came to anything. Amy used to call him 'half digit' because he only had half a middle finger on one of his hands. He still pestered her for some money she owed him for the snacks for the vending machine. Amy was adamant, he wasn't going to get one single penny from her after he had conned her into a six-year lease when they had verbally agreed on a year lease! He of course wouldn't take her to court because he knew he would end up in prison for fraud."

The detectives glanced at each other; both of them knew they had a possible suspect.

"Did Amy have a mobile phone?" asked DI Johnson.

"Oh no, she wouldn't have anything like that, she didn't like being interrupted while she was gardening. I only have a simple one for emergencies, my grandson insisted I should have one in case I had a fall," Fora told them. She lifted out her own mobile phone from her pocket to show them.

"What about all the lodgers she had, was there any trouble with them?" DCI Crawford wanted to know.

"There was only one," Amy replied. "He did a moonlight flit without paying his rent, I can't remember the full story but she eventually found him and took him to court and got her money back."

The rain was violently sheeting it down, it was so loud they all had to raise their voices to hear one another.

"What was his name and address?" continued the detective in his line of questioning.

"Oh, I've no idea, she'll have written it down somewhere, she always does," came the reply.

"Is there anyone else you can think of who could have killed her?" asked the DI.

"I wouldn't have thought anyone would have wanted to kill her, she was such a lovely person, she was kind to everyone. Mind you, if you crossed her, she would have you in court in no time at all! She was hot on justice," replied Flora, nodding her head.

Flora was asked – "Where were you yesterday afternoon, we have to ask to eliminate you from our inquiries."

"I was at the dentist down the street and then I went shopping," answered Flora, certain of her whereabouts.

"We are grateful for the information and your time, if you think of anything else let us know, here is my card – ring the number at the bottom." The DCI handed her his card and smiled.

The detectives left and strode out of the flats to their car parked on the roadside. The rain had stopped as suddenly as it had started. They sidestepped the puddles left after the storm – the drains were struggling to cope with the quantity of water flowing down the road and some of the pavements were flooded.

The DI, deep in thought, stated, "It's amazing when we start to investigate crime, it's like a window opening up onto people's secret way of life, we are all so different."

"Amy certainly had an unusual way of life!" exclaimed his colleague. "We'll go back and sort out these files, see if we can create a list of suspects." A fading rumble of thunder could be heard in the distance; the storm had moved on.

The office at the police station was very hot and humid even with the window open, there was no air conditioning; the storm had failed to clear the air. They sat reading the files, occasionally one of them would chuckle at Amy's humorous comments.

"Found him, the lodger who she treated like a son, he lives around the corner from here – Paul White," DI Johnson remarked.

His senior colleague replied, "We'll interview him as soon as possible."

It was a long evening sorting through the files, they had a takeaway and drinks brought in. The air was cooling down making the task easier as the evening wore on.

"Here's our final list, the lodger; she treated as a son – Paul White – we will have to question him to eliminate him from our inquiries. The lodger who she took to court – Steven Robinson – for doing a moonlight flit and not paying his rent. The Vending machine man – Stuart Wilson, or 'half digit' as she called him. Paul White's landlord – Jeff Thompson. The amorous man pestering Amy – Tony Davies; I don't think it will be him, he rung while we were in the office but we will have a word with him; they are all potential suspects," DCI Crawford announced.

"Jeff Thompson, how was he involved with Amy?" asked the DI.

"Apparently Amy was helping Paul White with a small claims court application against his ruthless landlord, Paul had to move out of his apartment due to a rat infestation problem and his landlord wouldn't compensate him for the rent he'd already paid for the following month. The landlord, Jeff Thompson, told Paul he had another three months left on his contract! Amy made a good case against Jeff Thompson; she had inspected the premises herself and gave a proper written statement, signed and dated. Amy had also taken dated photographs to back up their case. It's possible the landlord could have killed her out of revenge as his rental apartments were shut down, it was a huge loss of income for him."

The following morning, the detectives walked around the corner to interview Paul White. He lived in a small semi-detached house on an avenue off the main road. The detective chief inspector knocked on the glass door; a white bearded male in his 30s answered.

"Am I speaking to Paul White?"

"Yes, you are," came the casual reply.

"We are here to ask a few questions about Amy Lewis,"

the detective informed the half-dressed male who was standing at the opened door. After the introductions, the detectives were invited into the house.

"Come in, we were just getting dressed, would you like a coffee?" Paul asked in a kind voice.

"No, not for me thank you," the detectives replied in unison.

"Who is it, Paul?" shouted a young female voice from upstairs.

"It's the police, about Amy," came the reply. Paul turned to the detectives. "Come and sit yourselves down in here," Paul suggested, leading them into a brightly painted lounge away from the hallway. A black and white cat inquisitively strolled into the room and sat washing its face with its black paw.

"We have the sad news that Amy was found murdered yesterday at her property," began DCI Crawford.

Paul glanced over to the detective with sorrowful eyes. In a low mournful tone of voice, he replied, "I heard she had been murdered, I was absolutely devastated to hear the news; I couldn't help but cry. We had a special bond did Amy and I. She was like a caring, loving mum to me; she was always ready to help me."

"When did you last see Amy?" he was asked.

Paul began to think – "About a week ago now, I was helping her string up some herbs onto hooks in her walk-in pantry while we caught up on our news. She was a little bit eccentric! I loved her for that." Paul chuckled. "I should go around and water and feed the hens and attend to the greenhouse and garden, it was her pride and joy you know… it's the least I can do for her now."

"I'd be very grateful if you could do that until everything is sorted," replied the DCI. "Tell us how you met Amy and a bit about her – her habits and where she went and who she saw, to give us an idea of her way of life."

"She took me in as a lodger on short notice," Paul was pleased to explain. "I thought she was exceptionally kind to do that. She even helped me take my previous landlord through the small claims court! I managed to get all my money back! The apartment building was converted from an old mansion, where I used to live – it was infested with rats! It was a total nightmare and my landlord wouldn't give me my money back, you know, the advanced rent I'd paid him! The whole building was eventually forcibly shut down." Paul laughed. "Serves him right that he had no income coming in!"

"Did the landlord ever approach Amy on the matter?" Paul was asked.

"No, everything was done via the post or online through the court," Paul replied. "She did have a 4" nail stuck in her tyre on the passenger's side at the front of her car; this was shortly after the court case was finished. Amy thought it could have been my landlord seeking petty revenge. She also had a man ring her up from the council, accusing her of having another person living in the house when she was claiming a single occupancy discount. The man from the council claimed a member of the public had reported her. This was when she was living on her own after her husband died and hadn't any lodgers; I'd left by then. She decided to ring the council back and was told they hadn't rung her; she assumed it was my nasty landlord trying to frighten her."

Paul checked his watch and continued, "There was an old bowl full of snails left in her garden, that was another thing and a bag of dog poo slung onto her garden path, there were phone calls during the night too. They were only petty things really."

"Who did Amy associate with?" asked the DCI.

"Amy had her best friend Flora, who she called Flo. They had known each other for many years. Amy sometimes went to knitting and craft clubs in the village but mainly stayed at home tending to her garden and storing food. I'd never seen anything like it in her pantry!" He laughed again. The detectives were surprised how relaxed he was; however, they were grateful for his information, they thought Paul was a friendly, pleasant sort of person and could see why Amy had taken to him. "Did you know there are 30 different ways to use cider vinegar! Amy used to take my apple cores and shove them in a jar with water and sugar and shake the jar occasionally and let it ferment! She even ground up orange peel! There are tons of ways to use orange peel! Nothing was wasted with Amy!"

"Did she have any men friends?" DCI Crawford asked to speed up the interview and keep Paul on track.

"Yeah! I introduced her to dating online, she told me she was lonely. We used to go out together for the occasional meal but she really needed someone of her own age to talk to. I don't think she met anyone who was suitable on the dating website, she found it tiresome and time consuming going through all the male silver surfers on the online site."

"Did she tell you about anyone who she was afraid of or who had done her any harm?" Paul was asked.

Paul thought for a few seconds. "She was fed up with one persistent admirer, I know that much, but the others seemed harmless. She filled me in about when she had her tyres slashed; this was when she ran the coarse fishery and woods for picnicking. She told me she had had a few altercations with people breaking her rules! She had a gang of thugs who had surrounded her once, the gang leader was nose to nose with her – effing, blinding, and swearing at her – she said she was terrified but stood her ground and banned the lot of them; she was certainly a courageous woman!"

"Did they do anything for revenge?" queried DI Johnson.

"No, but I think the ringleader came back in disguise to fish the following season – it was the best coarse fishery in the area and he wasn't going to go elsewhere. Amy recognized him but his friends told her, he wasn't who she thought he was. He was allowed to stay as long as he behaved himself. He bent over backwards for her, helping her mend a gate and lifting a heavy pump out of the lake for her. She had that effect on people; she was kind but firm."

The DCI felt he was going off track and brought him back by asking, "Did she tell you about any other person she had bother with?"

"Yeah, the youth that was the lodger before me, Amy took him to court. He had signed a contract for six months. I know in my contract I could leave before then as long as I paid £100 towards advertising cost of the room and loss of income. This youth, Steven, I think he was called, moved out without paying the £100 and without giving proper notice! She got in touch with him on his mobile phone, he hadn't even left a forwarding address like his contract had stated he had to. She explained about the contract to him, but he stopped corresponding with her."

Paul drunk the rest of his coffee and continued – "Amy was determined to find him; the contract clearly stated that if the £100 were not paid within two weeks of him leaving, she had the right to charge for the rest of the six months' rent. So, Amy hired a private detective to find Steven. Apparently, he had lied about everything to her. Anyway, she found him living with his girlfriend and took him to court and won! He had to pay out a lot of money for abusing the contract, the private detective's fees, and the court fees!"

The DCI thought Steven definitely had a motive for revenge for murdering Amy. The cat strolled over to Paul and jumped onto his lap; he stroked her, while she curled up to go to sleep.

"Flora, or Flo, told us about a man Amy referred to as 'Half digit', can you tell us anything about him?" asked DCI Crawford.

Paul laughed. "Yes, 'Half digit', I don't know his real name. The first time I met him was when he came to Amy's house, I was working on my car on the back road. He was wanting some money she owed him. Amy told him straight, 'take me to court', and slammed the door in his face!" Paul chuckled to himself.

"Did he come often for the money?" the DI inquired.

"I think he usually rang her; she would say the same thing and slam down the telephone receiver. She told me, he would never get his money back and that he wouldn't entertain taking her to court because he had conned her husband into signing the document regarding leasing some vending machines. Apparently, 'Half digit' had been to see Amy's husband and had told him, 'Amy has approved the document and it just needs your signature to complete the deal'."

Paul caught his breath and continued, "Her husband not knowing he was a con man signed it! It meant that when Amy took 'Half digit' to court it was thrown out on technicalities because it was her husband that had signed up for the six-year lease, not her. Amy insisted in court, she had only agreed to a one-year lease and her husband was only supposed to be the guarantor. Her husband was seriously ill; so, he couldn't take the matter further, and then the poor chap died."

"When was the last time 'Half digit' came to pester her?" Paul was asked.

He thought for a moment. "I think Amy said he'd been around the week before, that was when I last saw Amy, so it would be about a fortnight ago." Paul's voice choked up with emotion. "Amy told me he sounded quite desperate!"

At that particular moment, a leggy young woman wearing faded blue jeans, cropped at the thighs, and a crumpled red top, walked barefooted into the room. She swished her long blonde hair from her face. Paul's eyes sparkled. "Here's my girlfriend, Josie. It's about time you surfaced, it's 10:15!" Paul remarked, grinning at her.

"Well, I didn't want to interrupt!" Josie exclaimed, smiling at the detectives.

"I'm glad you are here; we are asking this question to everyone. Where were you both on 18th August, in the afternoon, two days ago?" DCI Crawford asked.

The young woman glanced at Paul and replied, "We were both here, Paul and I are having a week's holiday from work."

"Where were you the following morning between five and seven?" asked DI Johnson.

Paul immediately replied, "We were in bed, we have a lie in every morning when we are on holiday."

"Thank you for all the useful information and for your time," the DCI replied. The two detectives saw themselves out of the front door and left the premises.

"What did they want?" asked Josie as she began to make a mug of coffee in the kitchen.

"They were asking about Amy and how she lived, who she knew – looking for suspects I suppose."

"Poor Amy, she didn't deserve to be murdered," Josie replied, turning towards Paul.

"No, she definitely didn't deserve it, she was a lovely, kind person. I loved her like my own mother, I shall truly miss her. I'll have to ask Flo when her funeral is, we will both go and pay our respects."

Josie nodded. "There will be a post-mortem and an inquest and all that, so it won't be soon, I wouldn't think."

Paul lay back on the sofa disturbing the cat from her slumber. He thought about the happy times he had had lodging with Amy, helping her in the vegetable and fruit garden; also learning about the many survival skills she knew.

'People depend on big corporations and government too much these days,' she used to prattle on. 'You don't need shampoo in plastic bottles destroying the environment! I've not used shampoo for years; you don't need it. Hot water and fingers running through your hair and a towel rub, it's all that is required! After all, other animals don't need shampoo! You don't need cleaning fluid in spray bottles either, they just litter our planet. You only need to use orange peel as a scrub and apple cider vinegar as a cleaner on a cloth, far less expensive than these ridiculous brand names!' He could hear the sound of her brisk voice even now; she spoke a lot of sense in many ways.

'What if there was a crisis, one of those electromagnetic pulses or something, that destroy the national grid! Then what? Most people can't live without electricity. There would be no deep freezers, fridges, TVs, lighting, or heating that would be working! There would be no electricity for the pumps; to pump the drinking water and sewage. People wouldn't be able to cope! You only need to bury a dustbin in the garden to have a cool place to store food. Most people don't even have a chimney or flue anymore, so they can't collect wood and burn their rubbish on an open fire to keep warm and cook food! You listen and you learn my ways, it may help you one day and you can teach others how to survive!' He thought she was a wise old woman.

"A penny for your thoughts?" asked Josie, entering the room from the kitchen; she was holding a mug of coffee in her hand.

"I was thinking about dear old Amy, what a character she was, she had this old world sussed out, a real survivor until... well you know. We should go to her place and feed and water the hens, there will be lots of produce to pick and the greenhouse will need watering."

****

The detectives arrived back at the police station; their team of officers had been going through the criminal records of all the suspects.

"Paul White has no criminal record but his previous landlord had a case of negligence. The vending machine man, Stuart Wilson, has had several cases of domestic abuse and violence reported; he's even had a short prison sentence. Steven Robinson, the lodger who did the moonlight flit, has been to court for petty theft and minor car offences."

"What about Tony Davies, the amorous man who was still pestering Amy?" asked DI Johnson.

"There are no criminal records that we can find," came the reply.

"It looks like Stuart Wilson, the vending machine man, is our main suspect up to now, we'll go and see him this afternoon – find out if he still has that small office on the trading estate, will you?" The DCI continued – "Have you found any link with these suspects to the pub murder?"

"Yes, Jane's brother told us that the two gaming vending machines in the pub, were also ordered from Stuart Wilson. Jane Hughes had complained to the leasing company that the vending machines ordered from Stuart were refurbished and not new. The leasing company had told them otherwise. The vending machines were the only link we've found to both murders."

"Mm, we may have cracked this case already, let's hope so," DCI Crawford assumed.

"Did you interview the wife of Jane Hughes' brother

before he arrived home from the pub?" DI Johnson asked the police officer.

"Yes, we did, she confirmed her husband's alibi – they were both at home in bed when Jane Hughes, his sister, was murdered at the pub."

"Was there any DNA found at any of the crime scenes?" queried the senior detective.

"No, not a damn thing up to now, forensics are still analysing the evidence, though. The murderer was either very careful or extremely lucky," the officer replied.

****

Paul and Josie arrived in their car and parked at the dead end of the back lane on the grass verge, near Amy's house and garden. In front of them was Amy's old car parked up. It was strange to Paul, to walk up the flagstone garden path knowing he would never see Amy again.

"You don't think the murderer will return, do you?" Josie asked in a scared voice. She was cautiously looking around to see if there was anyone about.

"I wouldn't think so, he's already killed his victim, why would he need to come back?" Paul asked.

Josie shrugged her shoulders, still not convinced.

"Hey look, there's loads of fruit. What are they?" asked Josie. She was beginning to pick them and placing them in the large plastic bowl they had brought with them.

"They're a type of strawberry, the plant doesn't grow

runners like normal strawberry plants. They are also more prolific and keep on fruiting until the frost."

"Ooh, you do sound knowledgeable, I'm impressed!" Josie grinned.

Paul laughed. "It's what Amy taught me, besides a lot of other things. Here taste one, they taste like bubble gum!"

"Mm... yes, you're right, they do!" Josie replied, chewing the small ripe strawberry.

"You carry on picking the strawberries and I'll water and feed the hens and the greenhouse," Paul suggested.

The hens were pleased to see some food and water arriving in buckets, they were running very low on fresh clean water. They ran to greet Paul as he opened the chicken wired gate. After scattering the grain onto the baked soil, to satisfy the hens, he checked the hen house for eggs. He was pleased to find eight large brown eggs.

There were tomatoes and cucumbers ready to be picked but the stalks and leaves appeared to be dying off from the lack of water. Paul noticed a stain on the sandstone slab in the greenhouse, near to the bench. The police had had a team around to the property, to clean up the blood, but obviously couldn't remove the mark completely. Blood smears in the house had also been removed. Paul stared at the dark stain for a moment; a reminder of Amy, the woman he called Mum. He felt extremely emotional and wiped away a tear trickling down his cheek.

"We can have a feast with all this food in the garden!" Josie exclaimed as she heard Paul returning. She picked another strawberry and placed it in her mouth.

"I'll pick some lettuce leaves; Amy grows a few different varieties in a few tubs. If you only pick a few leaves at a time they keep on growing and last the whole season. Same with the cabbage and kale. I'll dig up some onions too." Luckily Amy had left a bottle of water in the tubs; they were slowly dripping water into the tubs of lettuces or else they would have withered away in the heat.

"These runner beans, peas, and broad beans look ready, should we take these as well?" called out Josie as Paul walked away.

Paul looked around at the green products and smiled. "Yes, pick them, and I'll dig up some more potatoes as well."

When Paul arrived back to where Josie was working, he suggested they put everything in the bucket. Paul watered the whole garden before they decided to go home.

They left the garden laden with produce and headed towards the car. Paul glanced back over his shoulder to the white painted house, wondering who would inherit the property. He had no idea that Amy had left it to him in her will.

Paul and Josie arrived home late for lunch; they both prepared a lovely meal together. Paul wrapped his loving arms around Josie as she was washing the lettuce at the sink. Her blonde hair was combed into a large bun on the top of her head revealing her slender neck. He kissed her tenderly on the soft nape of her neck. She swung around and melted into his arms. Their moist lips touched, they kissed enthusiastically, his arms gripping her tightly around her slim waist. She slipped her hands under his T-shirt and caressed his warm, toned, tanned body.

Suddenly, his mobile rang out in his jeans pocket. "Damn it, just when I was enjoying myself, that will be my boss!"

Josie looked annoyed that his boss was taking preference to her when they were supposed to be on holiday. She carried on shaking the lettuce in the colander while Paul walked into the lounge talking into his mobile phone.

"Oh no! Can't it wait!" Paul shouted, irritated at being disturbed. His boss was explaining on the other end of the phone that he needed him at the office, he further explained they had been burgled and ransacked. "Oh... I'm on my way!" Paul replied with a sigh; he knew Josie wouldn't be happy.

Paul took Josie in his arms and kissed her on the cheek; he explained he had to go to the office at the garage where he worked – the place had been ransacked and money had been taken. He grabbed a cupcake to eat, to stop his tummy rumbling.

Josie was left alone with her thoughts. She was wildly in love with Paul and knew it wouldn't be long before he popped the question of marriage, it's what she had always wanted. He was the perfect guy for her; he had shown how loving and caring he was, not only with her but with Amy, the woman he called 'Mum'.

She knew she wouldn't be able to have a big wedding;

they were both constantly in debt with their credit cards maxed out. Paul didn't earn a big wage – they relied mainly on her income, to pay the hefty mortgage and the bills.

****

Flora had received a phone call from Amy's solicitor; she had asked Flora to collect some information for her for the probate. A list of furniture and valuables, bank statements, investment accounts and any other paperwork Amy possessed that may be important. Flora spent an afternoon at Amy's house collecting the information, *the furniture, her car, and her sentimental valuables wouldn't be worth a lot,* Flora thought to herself. Amy had told her where she kept her documents safe; they were stored in a fireproof metal box in the office – Flora had noticed they had been rifled through by the police. They hadn't been left neat and tidy like Amy would have left them.

While Flora was at Amy's house, she decided to wash up and leave the kitchen tidy; it was the least she could do for her dear friend. She checked the walk-in pantry and saw the muslin tied to the stool's four legs, with the stewed fruit on top; it had stopped dripping into the bowl below. *I better throw all that away, it's only going to go mouldy,* she thought to herself. She tidied up Amy's bedroom – the bed was stripped and the bed linen together with Amy's dirty laundry was taken home with her, to be washed and ironed – to be returned at a later date.

The Dilemma

Paul strode outside to his old light green saloon car; he was deep in thought. He didn't like being called back to work when he was on holiday; it was supposed to be his time. He slipped into his car and drove off. Perhaps his boss was blaming him for the theft! He became unsettled at the thought of having to defend himself from any allegations made against him.

He turned the corner and saw in the distance a police car parked near the garage. *Oh no*, he thought to himself, *was he going to be arrested on suspicion of theft?*

He pulled into the forecourt of the garage; he had worked there for two years as a mechanic. He strode out and entered the small garage shop. Hastily, he walked through into the office at the rear of the building. The room was in a total mess; desk drawers were open, papers were strewn around the room.

There stood a well-built policeman talking to Paul's

boss. Next to him stood his boss' 14 year old son. They all turned to see Paul striding through the doorway.

"We've found the culprit," his boss' strident voice boomed out. His son cowered looking shamefaced and guilty.

Paul asked in dismay, "What's going on?"

"Young Jimmy here has confessed to staging a burglary, making it look like an outsider had done it, then stealing the cash out of this secret drawer!" the burly police officer replied. "Well now I've cautioned him, there is no reason for me to stay." He walked out of the office leaving Paul astounded at Jimmy's behaviour.

"Sorry for dragging you out like this, Paul, I needed to get to the bottom of this, everyone was under suspicion! I rang the police straight away and then rang you. Jimmy came in later and confessed." Paul's boss sounded apologetic as he filled Paul in with the details. Paul could see the parental strain on his wrinkled brow. His boss continued – "I took the decision to have Jimmy cautioned, I hope he never does anything like this again."

"Jimmy, why would you want to steal from your own father?" asked Paul, stunned at Jimmy's actions.

"I wanted an electric scooter, like all mi mates have got. I knew Dad wouldn't give me one, so I took the money, I'm really sorry and I'll not do it again ever!" Jimmy replied full of remorse.

Paul's boss was emotionally distressed, he thought he had brought his son up, to know better.

"Jimmy, start tidying up this mess," his father sternly told him. "I'll have a word with Paul." He took Paul aside; he spoke in a milder tone of voice. "Look, I apologize for even thinking for a moment it was you, but I knew it was an inside job as who else would know where the money was hidden." Paul didn't know what to say but he was relieved he was no longer under suspicion.

"I'll see you on Monday, enjoy the rest of your holiday and give my regards to Josie," his boss cheerfully told him.

"Yeah, OK, I'll see you then," Paul replied as he walked away; he could hear his boss scolding his son in the background.

Paul was uneasy as he drove home; he wasn't happy he'd been suspected of a crime he had not committed. He would never steal from his boss; he became quite angry at the thought of what could have happened if his boss' son hadn't owned up to his looting. A furrowed brow and tense stature resulted in his negative thoughts.

"That was quick, why are you looking so tense? You look as if you've been fired!" Josie exclaimed as she turned to greet Paul walking into the kitchen. Her furrowed brow and strained smile showed a look of concern on her face.

Paul sounded annoyed when he spoke, he told her – "My boss was accusing me of stealing, or at least I was under suspicion of doing so. His own son confessed to it all. A policeman was even there! He cautioned young Jimmy."

Josie gasped, "That wasn't fair to accuse you, you were here with me, on holiday!" Josie put the final dish of food on the kitchen table and beckoned Paul to sit down. Paul was subdued. Josie tried to lighten the atmosphere by chatting about Amy and her garden.

****

Back at the police station, the two detectives were preparing to go and interview the vending machine man, known as 'Half digit', at his office on the trading estate. They arrived at a small office with a large window; DCI Crawford knocked on the half glass door. Stuart Wilson could be seen sitting at his desk, concentrating on his calculations. He heard the loud knocks and looked up. He saw the detectives stood at the door; he knew them from other visits he had had. He stood up revealing his six foot tall sturdy figure. The detectives were invited in and were asked to take a seat.

After the customary introductions, Stuart Wilson asked in a polite but toneless voice. "Now, how can I help you?" The detectives immediately spotted the half digit on his right hand as Stuart placed his hands on his desk, to seat himself in his black office swivel chair.

"We are investigating two murders; we wish to eliminate you from our inquiries. Both of the women who have been murdered had vending machines that had been ordered from you. So, you will know them both – Amy Lewis out at Raystone and Jane Hughes from 'The Eaves' Pub at Blackendale. We believe you had recently visited

Amy Lewis as she had an outstanding payment owing to you; for items for the vending machines."

Without any flicker of surprise at the deaths of the two women; Stuart Wilson stated, "That's right, Amy Lewis does owe me money. I did go around to her house but she slammed the door in my face!" Stuart removed his black rimmed glasses from his face and rubbed his tired eyes. His distinctive, short curly, ginger hair on his square framed head made him a person you wouldn't forget.

"Where were you on the afternoon of August 18th?" one of the detectives asked.

Calmly Stuart Wilson checked his diary laid on his desk.

"I was at a meeting with the vending machine company from 1.30 to 4.30," he replied, looking up at the two detectives.

"Where were you the following morning between five and seven?" he was asked.

"I was in bed with my wife, Jackie," he replied with a smirky grin.

"We will be checking your alibi, so we can eliminate you from our investigation," stated the DCI.

"Feel free," Stuart replied, leaning back in his office chair, relaxing and raising his hands to clasp them behind his head. "I had nothing to do with these murders," he replied confidently.

The detectives left; they sat in their car discussing the meeting.

"He looked confident, maybe he is telling the truth,

we'll check out the vending machine company and interview his wife, Jackie. We go past his house, we'll pop in and have a word with her," the senior detective remarked. DI Johnson contacted base on the radio, to ask them to contact the vending machine company to check out Stuart Wilson's alibi.

The detectives drove on and parked in front of a row of Victorian houses with steep tree-lined driveways. They strolled up the incline and rang the ornate bell on the door frame. A timid, slender female answered the door. They could see she had a faded bruise around her left eye and recent bruising to her arms. After the introductions, DCI Crawford asked in a gentle voice, "Do you mind if we come in and ask you a few questions?"

Without a word the woman meekly led them into a large sitting room with a bay window; she sat down in a red wing backed armchair; the detectives remained standing. Out of the corner of their eyes, they could see their reflections moving in a huge mirror, mounted over the white mantelpiece. The fire had a cast iron surround with a hood; blue and white tiles were inserted into the sides.

DCI Crawford spoke first. "We are investigating two murders in the area, we have interviewed your husband, Stuart Wilson. We wish to check his alibi, to eliminate him from our inquiries. Where were you both on the afternoon of August 18th?"

The woman looked blank. "I don't know, what day was that?"

"Tuesday," came the immediate reply.

"I was here, doing laundry and Stuart was at work," she replied, nervously biting her lip; her hand was nervously stroking her ash blonde hair.

"What time did Stuart arrive home after work?" Jackie was asked.

"The normal time, just after six," she replied swiftly.

"Where were you both, the following morning between five and seven?" asked the DI, in a more abrupt way – he knew Stuart Wilson could have already contacted her about his interview and told her what to say.

"At that time in the morning, we would be in bed," Jackie replied submissively, lowering her pale blue eyes.

"How did you come by your bruises?" DCI Crawford asked in a gentler kind of way. The woman looked nervous and embarrassed; she fidgeted and replied with an uncertain tone, "Oh… I fell in the garden… it's nothing."

"Thank you for your information, we'll not take up any more of your time," the DCI told her, and the detectives saw themselves out of the premises. They walked along a sandstone tiled hallway and through the original Victorian stained glass door.

Sitting in their car, the detectives talked about the woman. "She looks as if Stuart Wilson has knocked her about a bit. Those bruises are the tell-tale signs of domestic abuse, I bet," DCI Crawford uttered with a sigh.

"Pity we can't do anything, it's up to her to report the abuse. I know the neighbours have phoned us in the past when they've heard Stuart Wilson being violent towards her. Our officers have been around a few times, I believe, to calm the situation down," his colleague replied.

"He's done time in prison for assaulting a man in a pub, not a very nice character," remarked the DCI.

A call came in: "The vending machine company, have verified that Stuart Wilson was at a meeting with them, at the time of Amy Lewis' murder."

"That brings us back to square one, Stuart Wilson was our prime suspect for both murders; now where do we go from here?" The lead detective was thinking out loud after the unexpected news. He continued – "The murders may not be linked with the vending machines, after all, they may be two separate murders or an opportunist desperately grabbing money where he could."

"If it was a random opportunist, it will make our solving of the cases a lot more difficult," the DI added.

****

After lunch, Paul and Josie travelled the short journey to Amy's property.

"I used to call her the doomsday prepper, you know!" Paul giggled.

"I bet she wasn't pleased with that title," Josie replied, jumping out of the car, holding a basket and a bowl.

"I think, she was quite proud of the fact that she was self-sufficient and a survivor, she seemed to know all the old ways of doing things," Paul remarked as he headed to the garden shed. Josie began pulling up a few onions while Paul dug up a few more potatoes using a fork. The potato tops were quickly dying back. The stems were folded over, knuckled, and gnarled with brown crinkly leaves.

Josie held onto the long onion stems and shook and swirled the onion bulbs in the water in the water tub, removing any soil stuck to the roots.

Paul found a large plant pot with holes at its base, and after Josie had finished, he threw the potatoes into the plant pot and submersed the plant pot in the water in the tub, and shook it, to clean the potatoes.

The hens were aware they had arrived and rushed to the fence hoping to be fed. "Buck, buck, buck," they called trying to gain attention. Paul washed out their poultry drinkers and refilled them. He scattered some mixed grain on the ground for them; the hens scrambled to peck up the grain, the rest he poured into the troughs inside the hen house. He collected the eggs laid on the straw in the wooden nesting boxes.

I hope the foxes keep away as I'm unable to fasten them in the hen house at night, he thought to himself. Amy had told him stories of foxes digging under the wire fence to get into poultry enclosures and indiscriminately kill the whole lot only to eat one. He stood for a moment in thought, he really liked this country life, being close to nature; he wished he could afford to buy Amy's place.

Josie began collecting the strawberries and other

vegetables that were ready to be picked.

"You had better water everything – the soil is so dry," Josie suggested. Paul turned the garden tap on at the house wall and purposefully sprayed the unsuspecting Josie with cold water. He was delighted with her squeals and laughter; she was so full of fun!

"I'll get you for this!" Josie warned through her vivacious laughter. The hot weather soon dried her clothing as they continued with their work.

After their jobs were finished, Paul announced, "I'll show you the house, I know where the spare key is."

"I don't think we should go in," Josie replied, surprised at his suggestion.

"Well, we'll look through the windows then," Paul proposed instead.

Paul pointed out to her the bedroom window where he used to have a room in the days when he lodged with Amy. Josie could see the floral printed curtains hung at each side of the small window. Paul told her how happy he had been, living here.

Josie pressed her nose against the living room window to look inside. She turned to Paul and was about to speak when he laughed out loud. Josie, curious as to what was so hilarious, demanded – "what are you laughing at?" with a glint in her eye.

"You look so cute with the spot of dust on the end of your nose!" Paul shrieked with laughter again.

"I was just about to say, what a lovely cosy living room

Amy has." She playfully hit Paul on the arm and ran. Paul ran after her, he soon caught her and gently dragged her to the shed; they were both giggling and laughing. Once inside the shed, he passionately held her tightly and his precious kisses alighted on her soft lips. She responded and curled her bare suntanned arms around his neck. She felt so in love with Paul, he was everything to her, he filled her soul with peace and contentment.

"It's a good job Amy doesn't have neighbours nearby; they would be wondering what we are up to!"

"To hell with the neighbours, it's just you and me." Paul lovingly caressed her warm body while kissing her cheek and neck with love and tenderness; Josie cherished every moment.

"I love you; you mean everything to me; you know that, don't you?" Paul questioned, softly whispering in her ear.

"I know," she tenderly replied. "I love you just as much and even more."

"Will you marry me, Josie?"

There was a pause, then Josie laughed. "I thought you would never ask! Of course, I'll marry you, I've waited for this precious moment for a very long time." Josie began kissing him so lovingly, it made Paul feel ecstatic!

"Who's there?" shouted an angry voice.

Paul and Josie quickly uncoupled. Paul strode out of the shed to face the person standing at the garden gate. Josie followed on nervously behind, *he could be the murderer;* she quietly wondered to herself.

The grey-haired man stood at the gate, looking stern; he had a walking stick held menacingly in his hand. The sight of that alarmed Josie, she was glad Paul was there to protect her.

"I'm Paul, I was a close friend of Amy; who are you?" Paul demanded to know.

"Oh, I see now, it's Paul the lodger, Amy spoke very highly of you. Have you come to keep the place going? I live down the lane," he lifted his stick and pointed in that direction. "I heard a commotion, so I came to investigate." The man's demeanour had changed, he was speaking in a kinder voice towards them.

"Yes, I'm keeping the place going until everything is sorted out; it's the least I can do, the police know I come here," Paul replied.

"I thought it was some kids come to wreck the place, sorry I disturbed you." The man started to briskly walk away.

"Thanks for checking and looking out for the property, we'll be leaving soon," Paul shouted after him, politely thanking him. The grey-haired man extended his arm upwards to give a wave, he adjusted his cap and vigorously walked down the lane.

"Come on, we'll go too," Josie uttered. She suddenly felt uneasy and afraid, in the open garden. They gathered up the rest of the products into the basket and strolled towards the car.

"I wonder what will happen to the old place," Paul

pondered, swishing his long fringe back off his face.

"It will probably be inherited by Amy's nearest relative; I would think. Then they will probably sell it." Paul didn't look pleased with that suggestion.

****

At the police station, the detectives were discussing the murder cases in a small office; the window was partly open, allowing a warm breeze to circulate the room. Papers and files filled the desktop only allowing enough room for the computer and the keyboard. A telephone and printer were sat on another table with coloured trays stacked vertically. Papers were piled up in the different coloured trays.

"I was sure these murders were going to be Stuart Wilson's doing, he had the profile. I wonder if the pathologist is absolutely certain of the time of death. He had confirmed it was mid-afternoon. The body was in the greenhouse on a boiling hot day, it took approximately 24 hours to find Amy. She could have deteriorated quicker than normal in that heat." The DCI wondered aloud. He sat down in an office chair, folding his arms, and pondered further.

The DI replied, "He will have accounted for that but we'll keep an open mind on that one – Stuart's Wilson's partner mentioned 'he was at work that afternoon' – but work for him is travelling around in his car seeing clients. At the time of death, we were given, Stuart was supposed to have been in a meeting with the vending machine company. So, he would have travelled quite near to Amy's place to get to the meeting, and then there was his return journey home."

"See if we can obtain any CCTV footage of his car in the area; it will give us an idea of the time he was travelling about in his car," his colleague suggested, looking thoughtful with a furrowed brow. "We must find a link to these two murders; perhaps Amy and Jane knew each other somehow."

"Or did they know a person who linked them?" the DI questioned. They continued bandying about ideas back and forth.

The young detective continued – "We should interview these other suspects to see if they were in the area that afternoon; if they were not, we can eliminate them from the investigation."

"Yes, we'll pay a visit to the lad that did a moonlight flit first and then Paul's last landlord – that Amy made a good court case against. I don't think the men she dated would have murdered her, but we'll interview them and see if they have strong alibis." The DCI closed down his computer and turned to his junior detective.

"What do you think about the murder at the pub?"

"If we don't find a link; it's looking more like an opportunist; he probably saw Jane Hughes pulling into the car park and thought there could be money in the till to steal. Perhaps he wasn't a local and didn't know the pub was empty – ready for the passing over to the new owners. Somehow the person had to end up killing her for some reason – perhaps she recognized him?"

Alex replied, "I will contact the National Crime Agency to see if we can arrange for some help with these cases before the murderer kills again. The behavioural analyst can give us a profile of the killer and the geographical analyst can give us the likely area where the killer lives. That's assuming there was one killer for the two murders. The experts could put us right on that. We'll also have all the blue estate cars checked out in the area as one could be connected with Jane Hughes' murder."

An officer walked in at that moment. "The superintendent wants a word with you both."

The detectives glanced at each other and walked towards the door; they knew he would be anxious to be updated on the cases.

****

Paul and Josie had arrived home. Josie was tremendously excited Paul had proposed, they had eagerly discussed their wedding plans on the journey home. It was all Josie wanted was to marry the man she deeply loved and to have his children.

They opened the back door and walked into the modern fitted kitchen; Josie laid the basket of fruit, vegetables, and eggs on the side. Paul approached her from behind and encircled his arms around her slim waist, he kissed her lightly on her blonde hair. Josie's eyes were sparkling, she adored his warm embraces. She turned to see his familiar, wide grin and romantic bright blue eyes. She pressed her moist lips against his, closing her eyes, she felt the warm loving sensations filter through her body.

Paul gently took her hand and walked her through the lounge to the hallway and up the sandy coloured carpeted stairs to the landing. All of a sudden, he lifted her off her feet, cradling her in his strong muscular arms. Josie squealed and laughed with pleasure. Paul carried her over the threshold of the bedroom and delicately laid her on the soft duvet.

He gently removed her clothes – a coloured T-shirt and blue shorts; he quickly removed his own clothes, the surge of love was filtering through the air, eagerness was building. They made love like nothing they had experienced before, love was circulating through their throbbing veins, streaming into their racing hearts, it was utter heaven as they slid into a peaceful relaxed pose. They quietly lay side by side smiling; their breathing was heavy in this serene energy of happiness.

****

A man in his 30s arrived home one night from work; he had finished eating a takeaway from the local Chinese place. He was a loner, absorbed in his work by day but often had murder on his mind by night. He made himself a coffee and stared at the blue and white tiled kitchen wall in a blank evil stare. His face was drawn and pale; *kill, kill*, a voice in his head shouted continuously. He had managed to suppress this 'other self' as he would refer to this evil voice – until recently.

Long ago when he was a small child, he desperately wanted to kill his drunken, aggressive and violent mother. Thoughts of how to go about it entered his little head, a stabbing – no, she may resist and he was not yet strong enough to overpower her. Push her downstairs, did he have the strength? His 'better self' would rein in these wicked thoughts... until the next time. He found relief in a violent fantasy world of drawing cruel monsters ripping people he hated to pieces with their powerful jaws full of razor-sharp pointed teeth.

At school he was bullied relentlessly, he hated being humiliated and degraded. His voice within his mind would scream – *kill, kill, kill*. He would have loved to have turned into a huge scaly, monstrous dragon; rearing up before them with rows of teeth like a shark to horrify them; breathing fire from his flared nostrils, consuming their bodies with flames and burning them all to a cinder.

There was a male English teacher at his school he particularly hated; the teacher used to pick on him nearly every English lesson. His 'other self' would scream inside him, *kill, kill, kill*. He would have laughed to see this overconfident, bully of a teacher, bent over double with a knife stuck in his stomach, blood pouring out from his wound; he would have twisted the knife again and again if he could, to get his full revenge.

Thoughts like this came rarely as a child, later the evil thoughts were more frequent as he became a teenager; adolescence was a constant battle of good over evil. His 'better self' had an immense task at stopping this evil creeping into his everyday thoughts. Even when he was casually walking down the street; he would be jolted with a sudden urge to kill! His 'other self' would become outraged at something he'd seen like a mother hitting her child. Anger and rage would well up inside him of the memories of his own abuse, until he was on the verge of insane acts, each time it was becoming more and more powerful, his 'better self' had less and less power to diffuse this monster building up inside his head.

His thoughts began to stray, to a few nights previous, the monster inside him had been triggered by a violent film he had watched into the early hours, the battle to control his 'other self' was lost. The tipping point had been reached; it was no longer a case of killing the people who were bad to him, it was killing whoever he could to gain supreme dominance. He drove around looking for revenge on anyone whom his 'other self' thought deserved to die. He drove on and on aimlessly around the villages seeking an unsuspecting victim; he was trying to avoid CCTV cameras in the town. He was driven by all the sheer hatred he had accumulated for many years. It wasn't until about

5.45 in the morning he saw a lone female victim pull into a pub car park. He pulled over by a tall garden wall about 100 metres from the pub. His heart was racing, he felt exhilarated; the time was drawing near to a kill – would it release all the pent up hate and set him free from this evil monster within him? He stretched his gloves on one by one over his trembling fingers.

He quickly ran to the opposite side of the road and watched the woman slip out of her car; she was searching for her key in her light brown shoulder bag. He watched her go behind the building, he walked casually into the car park in case he was being watched. His senses were on alert, he heard the key turn in the lock and the back door opening and shutting. He walked around the corner of the building to the back, just as he heard a vehicle travelling past on the road; the milk bottles were rattling in their crates. He noticed a skip parked in the car park at the back of the pub; he saw an empty bottle poking out from the rubbish piled high in the skip. He grabbed it, his eyes were darkening, his anger and rage were violently surging, he wanted revenge for all the pain he had suffered.

He opened the door in a heightened sense of euphoric murderous rage!

"What are you doing? You can't come in here," shouted the woman wearing a fawn-coloured skirt and jacket. Without a word, he sprinted towards her. Horrified, the woman quickly turned and started to run for her life. He soon caught up with her, he hit her violently on the back of the head with the base of the bottle. She fell to the floor; she was motionless at first, after a while, she gave out a blood curdling moan. The killer knelt down on one knee and repeatedly hit her with the bottle in the same place with all his anger and might; eventually the bottle broke. Shards and pieces of glass flew everywhere.

Electrified with this evil energy, he quickly scanned the room. He saw the keys placed in neat rows on the top of the bar and realized the pub must be changing hands. He saw her shoulder bag on a chair beside a table. He ran out with it searching for her purse. He found it – a red clasp purse; he squeezed the purse into his back pocket of his jeans and dumped the bag into the skip under some pieces of debris, and ran to his car. He could hear a dog barking in the distance. He removed his gloves and sat in the driver's seat, placing his bloody gloves on his knee; he wiped the blood off his face with a rag and drove off. He was relieved the deed had been done yet exhilarated with the adrenalin still rushing through his body, he was on an extreme high. His 'other self' was in complete control.

He pulled over when he thought he was safe and retrieved the purse from his jeans pocket with a handkerchief. He emptied the coins and a few notes onto the passenger seat and threw the red purse through his open car window, into the grass on the verge by the church.

When he arrived home, the excitement had started to wear off. His 'better self' was gaining control. He began to think about his vile deed, his 'better self' was scolding him about how evil he had been, he felt remorse and gut-wrenching guilt. He collected the blood-stained gloves, the rag, the handkerchief, and the driver's seat cover and cautiously walked into his home, with the bundle of evidence; he disposed of the items into a black bin liner. He lay on the sofa in a daze, it had all felt like a dream, *could it have really happened?* he thought; or was it all in his mind. Reality and fantasy had often merged in his head.

He walked into the bathroom; in the mirror he saw the plain truth – his reflection of himself stared back at him, showing him, he still had traces of blood on his face. He looked down at his T-shirt and arms; they were covered in blood splatter. *Had he murdered before,* he wondered? Had his 'other self' covered up the tracks before his 'better self' knew what was happening? He had a fragile grip on reality; he was so completely confused.

He stripped off completely and bungled the blood splattered clothes and trainers into the bin liner and stuffed that into a blue rubbish bag. He took a shower to remove any evidence of the brutal murder. On his way to work that morning, he dumped the blue bag of evidence into a pile of other blue rubbish bags – he was lucky that it was collection day, for the rubbish in the area.

The Ex-lodger

After work, the two detectives stopped at their favourite pub – 'The Farmer's Arms' – to relax before going home. It was full of people – it was a popular pub with the locals. A typical country pub with the old fashioned bar and benches lining the walls with wooden tables and chairs down the sides of the room.

"I'll get this round," the DI suggested, pulling out his wallet to retrieve his credit card.

"Thanks, Sam, my usual please," Alex, the DCI replied; he strolled over to a table with chairs nearby. He felt tired as he took a seat; he slipped off his gold coloured frame glasses to rub his sore eyes. He was a clean shaven man, tall in stature, with balding wavy mousy brown hair that was turning grey. He would be retiring soon hopefully; however, his greatest desire was to see these murders solved first and the killer or killers behind bars.

"Here you are, Alex, get that down yer, it will do you

good." They both smiled at each other. The two of them had been good friends for many years, Alex and his wife, Verona, treated Sam like one of the family. He was often invited for dinner at their comfortable detached house with its magnificent large garden, immaculately kept by his enthusiastic 'green-fingered' wife. Alex and Sam would also go to football matches together, they enjoyed each other's company at work and outside of work. They tried not to talk about their cases after hours unless it was a very serious clue that needed discussing; together they enjoyed making an excellent working team.

They sat talking for a while before becoming distracted by a man walking into the pub. He was tall with black rimmed glasses and a half finger on his right hand, his square head with his short red curly hair made him stand out amongst the other drinkers. The man, Stuart Wilson, noticed the detectives as he sauntered to the far end of the bar.

"How do," he muttered, acknowledging their presence. Both detectives nodded back in reply.

"This must be Stuart Wilson's nearest pub," Sam quietly remarked.

"Mmm, we know he is familiar with 'The Eaves' Pub at Blackendale as well, he had also met Jane Hughes the landlady who was murdered there as she ordered those vending machines from him," Alex replied. "Poor woman, they say she was selling up to start a new life, she never even got the chance. You never know when you are going to go, best live life to the full, 'er Sam."

"You're right there, Alex, could happen any time. No one knows when their number is going to be called."

The following morning a report was ready for them at the police station. The night shift had viewed and scrutinized a few tapes from CCTV cameras which had been collected from the area near to Amy Lewis' house and near to the pub in Blackendale, where Jane Hughes was murdered.

"We didn't find any of the suspect›s cars apart from Stuart Wilson's car being driven in the area between 12.59 and 1.26 pm and then around six pm, he wasn't found to be near Jane Hughes' pub the following morning."

The lead detective realized there was a time span not accounted for. Stuart Wilson had stated he was in a meeting from 1.30 to 4.30 pm, it would have taken him half an hour to arrive at Amy's property, avoiding the CCTV cameras, that would leave an hour between five and six pm when he could have committed the murder and travelled home.

Alex frowned. "Did the body of Amy Lewis deteriorate more rapidly than was thought and therefore the time of death could have been later in the afternoon around five or after?" He was thinking out loud. "We will definitely have to keep an open mind on that one."

The two detectives set off to interview Amy Lewis' ex-lodger, who in the past had done a 'moonlight flit'. They pulled up in front of a small bungalow. The wooden gate was in disrepair and the front garden was overgrown with weeds in the sun-baked lawn. A vehicle was parked there, covered in a green tarpaulin, held down with ropes and stones. Old tyres and wood littered the area. Sam, the DI, knocked on the door of the porch.

A little old woman opened the shabby door; her white hair was greasy and unkempt. Her bifocals had slid to the end of her sunburnt, peeling nose, she peered over the top of her spectacles with aging, clouding eyes.

"What do you want?" she asked sharply – she was disgusted she had been disturbed.

"Is Steven Robinson available to speak to? I am DCI Crawford and my colleague is DI Johnson. We would like to eliminate Steven from our inquiries."

She immediately turned. "Steven! Steven!" she shouted in a loud, hoarse voice.

Steven returned an abrupt answer back, from a bedroom at the back of the bungalow.

"What!"

"Someone's 'ere to see you," she shouted abruptly and scurried into the lounge, slamming the door behind her.

An unassuming character appeared in the corridor heading towards the front door; he slovenly dragged his feet as he walked towards them. Steven looked puzzled at the detectives who introduced themselves and repeated what they had told the old woman. Steven stood slouching, a small lad with an abundance of light brown curly hair. His old jeans were frayed, they had been cut off at the thighs; his red T-shirt clung tight to his skinny torso.

"Who was the old woman who answered the door?" asked the senior detective in an encouraging soft voice.

"She's my girlfriend's gran, she owns the bungalow, my girlfriend and I live here to help support her," the lad replied, still looking confused.

"Are you aware that Amy Lewis was murdered on Tuesday 18th August?" the DCI Crawford asked, which helped clarify to the lad the reason why they had come.

"I did hear about it and it was in the newspaper," Steven replied, slurring his words and lowering his eyes in a guilty fashion.

"We believe she took you to court for leaving your lodgings and not adhering to your lodger's contract. Is that correct?"

Steven looked surprised that they knew so much. "Yeah, I paid up though, I don't owe her nothin' more!" he pleaded in a throaty voice.

"Where were you on the afternoon of the 18th August and the following morning between five and seven?" he was abruptly asked.

"Dunno, I'll have to ask my girlfriend." He turned and shouted – "Jinnie, where were we on the afternoon of the 18th August?"

The detectives could hear his girlfriend replying in a loud ringing voice, they could hear everything she was saying.

"You remember we went over to the coast and sunbathed, it was scorching hot and you got sunburnt;

the car broke down on the way back. Remember now?" his girlfriend asked. She was a bit surprised he hadn't remembered. "The following morning, we had a lie in, exhausted from the day before," she added.

"Aw, yer, I remember now, I thought it was Wednesday when we went on our trip," he shouted back in reply.

"We were at Scarborough for the day," Steven told the detectives more confidently. "My car broke down, so we got a mate to tow us back home."

"What is your mate called and what is his mobile number?" he was asked.

"Mikey, just a mo – I'll get his number off my mobile." He retrieved his mobile phone from his creased jeans pocket and searched for Mikey's number.

Steven quickly read the number on his mobile phone screen; the DI was copying the number onto his own mobile phone, then he stepped back to make a call to Mikey. DCI Alex Crawford asked Steven where he worked.

"I'm unemployed at the moment," came the meek reply.

"Does your girlfriend work?" the detective asked.

"No," was the short response.

The DI finished the call with Mikey and stepped forward.

"Well, you're in the clear, Mikey has corroborated your story, a good mate to tow you back all that distance."

"Yeah, he's a good mate," Steven sullenly replied.

The detectives left convinced Steven wasn't involved.

"He seemed a bit of a dopey lad, couldn't see him

murdering anyone!" Sam remarked.

"It's more like Grandma is supporting them not the other way around," Alex suggested; they both laughed. "Don't forget tonight, seven sharp, remember, my wife and I are having a barbecue and she will be very disappointed if you don't turn up."

"I'll definitely be there, I'll bring some beers," Sam replied, grinning.

****

In the village shop in Raystone a group of women were stood gossiping.

"They haven't found the murderer yet," a large woman remarked, in a booming voice; she was standing next to a rack, full of colourful birthday cards. "I'm scared to even go to my shed in the garden now in case he's skulking around somewhere, I hope they catch him soon, my nerves are frayed."

A taller, skinny middle-aged woman with a lot of makeup on her face queried, "I wonder why he wanted to kill Amy? Poor dear; she wouldn't have much to steal, she lived quite frugally." The woman bent down to pick up a local newspaper from the bottom shelf and tucked it under her arm, in order to retrieve her purse from her cardigan pocket.

"It was probably an outsider, I keep my distance from any strangers now, you never know what they're here for," replied an elderly lady brushing away a fly buzzing around her wrinkly face.

"Well, Ada, you do right, keep your doors and windows locked as well, you never know," the large woman remarked; her eyes were wide with fear. "No one knows who this killer is, he may even be your neighbour!"

"It makes it even worse when there was that other murder at Blackendale – Jane Hughes, poor woman, just about to start a new life as well!" the shop assistant mentioned, joining in the conversation from behind the counter.

Another woman joined in – "I bet it's a serial killer on the loose, no one is safe now, I won't go anywhere without my dog, Max. I'm quite confident he wouldn't tackle me with my size and my faithful dog by my side." The overweight Jack Russell terrier looked up, recognizing his name, his sorrowful eyes pleading for a drink. He was panting in the heat, saliva dripping from his tongue; he tugged on his lead, he wanted to be outside.

"Here, Vera, I'll get your dog a drink, he looks overheated," the shop assistant suggested. She hurried to the back room to fetch a bowl of water and placed it in front of the terrier. The dog was pleased to see the bowl coming, he wagged his tail; his head immediately went down to lap up the cold refreshing water.

"You should get yourself a dog, Ada, living in that cottage away down that lonely lane; don't you be going out into the garden on a morning feeding them birds, the murderer might be waiting," the tall, skinny woman warned.

"That's a thought, I should throw their food out of the window, I'll not go out until he is caught now, but I had to get my pension and food in today."

"I'll walk you back, Ada; I don't want to see you harmed," suggested the large woman with the dog.

"Thank you, Vera; you are very kind," Ada replied with a smile.

Fear was rife in the two villages and the surrounding area; mothers were keeping their children indoors. They would rather cope with the squabbling of the restless children than have a murdered child.

****

"Wonderful to see you," Alex's wife, Verona, called out to greet Sam as he entered the large garden. Sam handed over the cans of beer; he saw there were about a dozen people there, milling around talking to each other, all casually dressed as he was. He was relieved: gatherings like this were really not his scene.

Alex walked over, grinning; he was pleased Sam had arrived on time. "I'll introduce you to the crowd, come and meet Alan, the accountant from Carlisle and his lovely wife Sue." Alex continued to introduce him to a judge, a vet, a doctor, and a solicitor together with their spouses. Sam mingled with the guests, chatting politely; he felt he was the 'odd one' out, being single, until a woman of his own age arrived late.

"So sorry I'm late, I was held up by a client." She was casually dressed in jeans and a long sleeved white top, slightly off the shoulder revealing her glowing suntan and a lace bra strap. Sam was immediately interested in this confident, tall brunette.

"Sam, come and say hello to Annette," Alex's wife called out.

Sam was stood by a tree watching Annette talking to Verona. He smiled and casually walked over to her, holding his pint of beer in one hand.

"Annette is one of our neighbours," Verona informed him. She turned to Annette and asked, "You are into real estate, aren't you?"

"Yes, I'm a property developer. How do you do, Sam," Annette replied turning towards him.

Sam cleared his throat with a little cough and introduced himself as a detective inspector, they began to chat – it came naturally to them as if they had known each other for years. He loved her smile and twinkling blue eyes.

"Grab a plate, everyone, tuck in while it's hot," shouted Alex, standing by the barbecue.

The garden was decorated with rows of coloured Chinese lanterns strung from tree to tree. The garden borders were covered with various types of plants, mostly in full bloom, radiating their vibrant colours out into the rays of light from the Chinese lanterns. The meat was sizzling on the large charcoal barbecue, emanating a wonderful tantalizing smell of barbecued medallion steaks and appetizing sausages. On the wooden tables were cut glass bowls of mixed salads and various delicious finger foods. Verona carried out of the kitchen a large stainless steel tray piled high of baked potatoes taken straight from the oven. The guests all filled their plates and sat on benches around the colourful, glowing garden. Alex walked around filling the ladies' glasses with wine. He was wearing a chef's hat and a white apron – he was in his element pandering to his guests' needs.

Sam began to relax with his newfound friend. She was interested to hear how he became a detective and his many adventures in the police force. Sam told her, he had always been interested in the law, from a young age, he was determined to stop violence and disorder in society. He was impressed with what Annette had to say, he admired Annette's business acumen and success, she was extremely good at her career.

The following day, Alex and Sam met in the corridor at the police station.

"I thought it went well last night, what did you think?" asked Alex.

"It was fantastic! I enjoyed every minute," came the reply.

"Especially when you met Annette!" Alex added with a grin and a twinkle in his eye. Sam laughed.

"I walked Annette home last night, so she would be

safe; she has a lovely house, I've got her phone number now – she even texted me this morning to wish me a good day!"

Alex was pleased – "Sounds promising, I hope you find a lot of happiness together, it's about time you settled down."

"I've asked her out, so it's a start," Sam replied, grinning.

They walked into a meeting in the incident room with the two male profilers. There was a hum of voices chatting about the cases until the criminal profiler was introduced by Alex, the detective chief inspector. The profiler began to speak in a loud deep voice.

"My opinion is, from the information I've been given, that these two murders have been carried out by two very different people. My reasoning is that Amy Lewis was killed by a single blow to the back of the head, probably by someone she knew and trusted as she had turned away from her killer; she was not attempting to escape through the door at the opposite end of the greenhouse from where the killer had entered. Amy had turned to walk to the bench in the greenhouse, to carry on working, is the most likely scenario. She was struck down, probably due to an argument that Amy finished when she turned herself around. The killer would probably be enraged with that and struck her."

He cleared his throat and continued. "Jane Hughes, on the other hand, was viciously and repeatedly attacked with the bottle until it smashed into smithereens, a violent and frenzied attack. She wasn't expecting anyone at that particular time in the morning, according to her brother. The killer had gained access through the open back door with the intent to kill and rob her. The victim was probably running away towards the office after seeing him with a bottle in his hand." He paused for a second to catch his breath. "The office door had a slide lock on the inside of the door, she would know this and would realize she had the means to be able to lock herself away from harm's way. She would know, the key to the office door and the spare were already labelled, and placed on the bar top. She was desperately trying to escape to save her own life at the time, unfortunately, the killer caught up with her and she was struck from behind. Her killer would most likely be in his 30s, a loner, problems with parents when he was growing up, violence and abuse that sort of thing. It would be the killing that he – and I most definitely think it's a male – it would be the killing that he needed to do; to satisfy his lust for revenge, the robbery was probably an added bonus for him." He paused for a moment and continued.

"This man is extremely dangerous now; he'll be addicted to the adrenalin high of this kill and will most certainly kill again and soon." The officers began to talk amongst themselves as the criminal profiler stepped away from the front of the room.

A large map was pinned to a board; the geographical profiler stepped forward and was introduced. "Here is a map of the area," he began, stroking his short black beard. "Both killers, I believe, will live locally. Jane Hughes' killer is likely to live in this area." He pointed on the map to a place about four miles away from the pub; using a red hand pointer, circulating it on the board in a large circle. "He had to have come from this area to avoid the CCTV camera here and here and here, so he was definitely aware of them, he had done his homework beforehand and was scouting the area for a lone victim before anyone was about. Amy's killer, on the other hand, is most likely to have come from this area." Again, he pointed to an area a couple of miles in diameter from Amy's house. "There are no CCTV cameras on this route to Amy's house from here, not like this route and this other route here." Again, he pointed along the various routes with his hand pointer, stopping at every CCTV camera marked on the route.

"Thank you, that narrows it down quite a bit, we need a list of blue estate cars owned in this area, as a blue estate car was seen 100 metres from the crime scene at the pub." DCI Alex Crawford circled the area with a black pen. "We also need a list of all the people Amy knew in this area." Another black circle was drawn. The police officers began to disperse after the meeting leaving the two main detectives alone.

"Stuart Wilson or 'Half digit' lives in this circle – did he come back pestering Amy for the money she owed him? Paul White had informed us; Amy had told him – Stuart Wilson was quite desperate when he had visited her roughly two weeks before her death," Alex quizzed.

"It would fit if the time of death was after five

that afternoon when Stuart returned home from the meeting with the vending machine company," added his colleague Sam.

They both stood looking at the map on the board, pondering who could the killers be.

****

Heavy breathing was the first sign that adrenalin was beginning to surge in the killer's veins. The monster within him was awakening! His anger had been triggered by a violent video he was watching at his home after work, he felt full of hate, anger, and aggression at his past abuses he had suffered as a small child and the later bullying he had endured at school. His 'better self' was quickly losing control as his 'other self' was too strong to be subdued. He slammed his fist on the coffee table, creasing his face up in defiance. *Kill, kill, kill,* the voice in his mind continuingly repeated, the venomous words were blasting out in his thumping head. He was shutting out the real world and drifting into a fantasy world of an extreme need to control and have supreme power over someone's life. His pupils in his eyes were enlarging, making his eyes appear black. His thoughts of murder consumed him like an evil veil shrouding his mind. He had to find a victim... now!

He quickly jumped into his car; it was a dark night, there was no moon. He would try his luck in the supermarket car park as he had seen in the violent video he had just watched. He was wearing black jeans and a black hooded jacket, so he wouldn't easily be seen. There was plenty of cover of rhododendron bushes in the far corner of the car park – he'd noticed before, it wasn't well lit in that particular area either.

He had a job parking as the car park was full and he was trying to avoid any cameras. He managed to park his car on the side street, away from any CCTV cameras. He walked towards the darker end of the car park, in between the street lighting. He peered around to make sure no one was watching and slipped through a gap in the hedge to hide behind a bush. The excitement was escalating for another kill. His keen eyes sharply observed the people leaving the car park, one by one in their vehicles, only one car remained in that dark, lonely section now. The air had started to cool; he zipped the rest of his jacket up, mainly to hide his white T-shirt. He patiently waited, hoping it was a vulnerable woman and not a heavyweight man who would come back to the lonely car. He picked up a large jagged stone from the ground, with his gloved hand – a lethal weapon he would use for his kill.

Suddenly, his sharp hearing heard footsteps and trolley wheels turning; they were coming closer. Crazy with rage, his violence was surging within him, he gripped the stone tighter. A tall, leggy unsuspecting female was pushing the trolley towards the lone car. She opened the boot of her car. *This is perfect*, he thought to himself. He suddenly got a glimpse of her familiar face and long blonde hair – he knew her! It was Josie, the woman who owned a successful dress shop; he knew she lived with Paul White who worked as a mechanic at the local garage. He cautiously looked around to see if Paul was anywhere near or if she was shopping alone. He couldn't see him; he was in luck! The adrenalin spewed into his veins; his heart raced violently.

'What a catch' he thought to his evil self. He stepped out slowly with the stealth of a cat hunting; ready to pounce on its unsuspecting victim. He walked quietly towards Josie, who was totally occupied in lifting her grocery bags and other items from the trolley into the boot of her car and never noticed him creeping slowly towards her. He was heading to the back of her to strike her from behind as he had mercilessly done before. Totally focused, his hand was gripping the stone tightly in his hand, he was nearly in the exact position for the kill. Sweat was pouring down his brow; he wiped his forehead with his sleeve; his heart was pounding so loud and so fast, he thought she would hear it.

Suddenly a voice called out, "Josie, I managed to get them, here they are." It was Paul calling out; he held up a white plastic carrier bag to show her.

Josie turned around, ignoring the man dressed in black who was walking away from her. She called out to Paul, "Great, I'm glad you managed to get them."

The killer carried on walking, quickening his pace, he didn't dare turn to look at Paul, in case he was recognized. He tried to hide the stone in his gloved hand the best way he could. When he was out of sight, he threw down the stone with all his might in a fit of rage; it hit the dry earth and bounced with a spray of fine soil and landed near a bush. He was totally frustrated and full of anger; he felt sick with disappointment. He would have to find another unsuspecting victim very soon.

Another Victim

The killer drove to a deserted country lane and parked his car in a secluded lay-by. He locked up his car, climbed the steps of a wooden stile over the drystone wall, and descended down the steps on the other side. He continued to walk along the well trodden footpath in the grassy meadow. He could hear cattle moving about at the far end of the field. He was anticipating an unsuspecting walker would come his way *but perhaps it was too late now,* he thought to himself.

The footpath took him to a stone stile at the other side of the field, he squeezed through the narrow gap and down the stone steps jutting out of the wall, on the other side. He ended up standing on gravel, on an unmade road with a small, isolated cottage to his right. It was Ada's cottage, situated down the lonely lane away from Raystone village.

He could see the light on in the lounge and an elderly lady sat in an armchair, alone. The killer was breathing heavily again as his excitement mounted. He pulled his black hood over his head to help disguise himself. He tried the door handle to the porch door at the side of the cottage; the door was locked. He brazenly knocked on the glass door and waited patiently.

Ada was sat in her lounge, thinking it was time to get herself ready for bed when she heard the knocking. She wasn't expecting anyone at that time of night and immediately became suspicious. *I really should see who it is,* she contemplated to herself, *it could be a neighbour down the lane wanting help.*

She could see the tall dark figure stood outside her porch and became afraid; the recent murders had made her a lot warier.

"What do you want?" Ada shouted in a sharp voice; she wasn't going to attempt to open the door to this stranger.

The man spoke in a gentle voice – "My car has broken down, over there–" he pointed to the way he had come. "My mobile phone has no charge to ring anyone, please can I use your telephone?"

"No, go away, or I'll phone the police!" Ada shouted abruptly, lifting her own mobile phone out of her cardigan pocket; she felt terrified and very vulnerable and was going to ring a friend. The killer knew it was best he walked away; it was obvious, she wasn't going to let him in. He squeezed through the narrow gap in the stone stile and began walking back to his car; the excitement of another kill had turned to bitter disappointment. He looked up to the night sky, it was dark with a few stars twinkling through; there was a chill in the air. He heard the haunting hooting sound of a tawny owl nearby; the cattle had gathered in the middle of the meadow – they shied away from him as he walked past. He could smell and see their breath, clouding in the cooling air. A few of them spewed out a sloppy mess into cow pats on the ground, the warm unpleasant aroma drifting towards his nostrils. As he walked on, the curious young cows started to follow him, so he swung around and chased them off. The cows darted away, kicking up their cloven hooves.

He had nearly reached the other stile when he saw a large woman in green wellington boots and a light green coat. She was struggling to lift her overweight Jack Russell terrier dog over the wooden stile with her.

"Please, let me help you," he suggested politely. He quickly grabbed hold of the dog from her arms, before she could say anything. The dog barked and tried desperately to struggle free, it was snarling and attempting to bite him. Immediately, he threw the dog over the stone wall. The terrier yelped in pain as he hit the ground on the other side. The woman was horrified and knew instantly he must be the murderer.

Stunned, she stared at the killer. He turned towards her and suddenly pulled the petrified woman off the wooden steps of the stile; she fought furiously for her life and managed to slip from his grasp. She ran as fast as she could, encumbered by her large size. The killer seized a stone from the ground near the wall; he could hear the dog was still yapping at the other side of the drystone wall, and he knew he had to be quick before the dog raised the alarm. The terrier had tried to jump onto the first step high up on the wooden stile, but he couldn't manage it, he was too old and fat. Frustrated at not being able to help his owner, he stood yapping at the stone wall.

The killer swiftly ran after the terrified, vulnerable woman; his heart was racing, his breathing was quick. He was exhilarated with the chase to kill, he enjoyed running after this innocent woman. His mouth was open, gulping in the night air as he ran as fast as he could. He soon caught up with her with his lengthy strides. The frightened woman knew her time had come, she was engulfed in extreme terror and was giving out a half-whimpered scream as she ran as fast as her weight would carry her. The killer made a swing at her head with the stone gripped tightly in his hand. He managed to hit her forcefully on the head, and she fell immediately to the ground. Dazed and confused, she groaned and attempted to get herself up. The killer, without mercy, bludgeoned her to death on the back of her head, caving in her skull, until no sound came out of her mouth. He smiled; he had satisfied his insatiable lust to kill; he hurriedly threw down the blood stained stone and checked her pockets for any money, but there wasn't any, only her house keys.

He quickly looked around to see if anyone had seen this evil, audacious act. His lips curled into an evil smile; he had again got away with another murder; he swiftly ran back to the wooden stile. The yapping terrier dog was waiting for him. The killer picked up a large stone and looked over the wall at the yapping terrier looking up at him; he mercilessly dropped the stone to hit the dog on his head. The terrier saw it falling and quickly backed off. The killer was in a quandary now – how could he escape to his car without his ankles being bitten by the dog? He didn't want his blood left at the scene of the crime, for the police to obtain his DNA profile. He frantically started to throw large stones from the wall top at the dog. One made a direct hit on his hind leg; the dog yelped in excruciating pain and ran away limping badly.

Relieved, the killer hurriedly climbed the wooden steps of the stile and jumped down the other side. He ran to his car, hurriedly sat down, and sped off; he felt a thrill run through his body – 'mission completed'; his evil 'other self' laughed to himself. He arrived home, absolutely elated, this was the best killing so far. It was a long time before he could calm the adrenalin racing through his veins; he went over and over every minute detail he had made, reliving every exciting and thrilling moment; he thought the murderous chase was absolutely riveting! His 'better self' didn't gain back any control until the early hours of the morning, when subsequently, guilt and remorse finally set in. Would he ever be able to conquer this evil monster growing ever more powerful inside him?

The cattle in the field had milled around the dead

body, they had curiously sniffed at the motionless corpse, buffeting each other to obtain a better look, they sniffed her still lifeless body with their broad wet noses, defecating on the scene. Saliva drooled out of their mouths onto the light green coat. When their curiosity waned, they meandered away to graze, unaware they had destroyed the crime scene.

The following morning, a farmhand, travelling on his quad bike came to check on the stock in the meadow. He came across the grizzly, messy scene of the murdered woman. He was horrified – his immediate thought was she had been trampled to death by the cows in the field, as her clothing was splattered with cow muck and drool. The area surrounding her body was puddled in sloppy cow dung and trampled grass. He rang the police on his mobile phone and informed his boss. He decided to drive the cows out of the field into the adjoining field ready for the police investigation.

After a short time, which appeared endless to the farmhand, the police and ambulance arrived on the scene, a few police officers stayed on the lane. The farmhand watched at a distance as he saw the field being invaded by many police officers and the ambulance crew all clambering over the wooden stile and racing to the body in the middle of the field. The woman was pronounced dead at the scene. It was obvious from the state of the body that she had died some time ago.

The farmhand was questioned in detail; he gave his name and address and where he worked and was allowed to go back to work. It was still not clear how the woman had died as the deep wound to her head could have been inflicted by cow's feet trampling her head; she could have been knocked over by the inquisitive young cows as she walked through the field, perhaps? She had no identification on her to inform them who she was. One astute police officer noticed a stone several feet from the body, probably accidentally kicked there by the cows milling around the scene. The officer bent down to scrutinize it for any evidence. He could see traces of blood and hair embedded in it.

"Hey, this could be the murder weapon!" he called to the others. The vital evidence was photographed in situ and placed in an evidence bag and labelled. The whole crime scene was photographed and a detailed search was carried out; they were looking for any clues the perpetrator may have dropped. Finally, the messy, smelly clothed body was gingerly placed and zipped into a body bag, and taken to a vehicle parked on the road. One of the police officers had found some blood spots in the lay-by, but the police couldn't understand why there were large stones scattered around in the road. One of the stones was found to have blood congealed on it and blood-stained short hairs clinging to it.

The Jack Russell terrier, after its terrifying ordeal, had managed to limp to a house he knew, trailing his lead behind him. He cowered under the garden hedge. He was traumatized and terrified by the savage attack; he was in immense pain. He licked his bloody open wound on his back leg and lay down exhausted and slipped in and out of unconsciousness until morning arrived.

When the occupant of the house opened the front door to go to work the following day, the poor dog gave out a pitiful whimper for help. The man heard the distressing whimper and saw something lying under the hedge.

He didn't know what it was at first, but he soon realized it was a Jack Russell terrier and recognized the dog as being Max, a dog he knew well.

"What's happened, old boy, have you been hit by a car? You still have your lead on," the kind man questioned aloud.

His wife was coming out of the house. "What is it, John?" asked Julie as she locked the front door.

"It's Max, Vera's dog, he looks as if he's been hit by a car, but he's still got his lead on, I hope Vera isn't hurt."

"I'll give her a ring, she will be frantic he is missing, she'll be worried sick." Julie retrieved her mobile phone from her bag to call her friend.

John opened the boot of his car and gently lay the whimpering dog inside.

"There is no reply, I rang for ages thinking she may be still in bed. Although I think she could be out looking for Max, I suppose; we better go around to her house and make sure she's alright."

They drove the short distance to her house. Max was still whimpering in pain in the boot of the car, a pitiful sound that made them both feel very anxious. There was no reply to their frantic knocking on Vera's front and back door.

"I'll leave a note telling her we've taken Max to the vets, she'll see it on her return if I post it through her letterbox," Julie suggested.

"We better get the dog to the vet immediately, he is in masses of pain," John remarked. He was saddened at the dog's horrific condition. Blood had matted on his fur; John could see a broken bone protruding from the deep bloody wound.

"I do hope Vera is alright, perhaps she's in hospital after being hit by a car or something?" his wife replied anxiously.

"You drive and I'll ring the local hospital," John suggested... "No, Vera hasn't been admitted to the hospital," he told Julie, shutting down his mobile phone.

"Where could she be?" Julie asked. She was shaken up with the shock of not knowing where her friend was.

They drove to the local vets and left the terrified, tormented dog with them – *at least they will be able to give him something to alleviate the pain,* they thought.

****

The detectives were discussing the latest body to be found.

"A gash to the back of the head with a stone perhaps sounds like our murderer has struck again!" DCI Alex Crawford exclaimed; he was horrified another murder had been committed on his patch.

Sam, his colleague, looked thoughtful. "No money was found on the body; the killer could have taken it."

"There were no significant tyre marks found in the lay-by, it's been so dry and dusty, had it have rained like the other day there may have been tyre tread impressions to give us a clue. And what about the stones in the road and the bloodstains there, the short hairs on one of the stones – what was that all about?"

Sam replied, "Perhaps the woman was throwing stones at the perpetrator to fend him off and she hit him and that's why there is blood and hair on the stone in the road."

"That would give us a DNA profile of the killer!" Alex exclaimed. He was starting to become excited that at last, they may have a clue about the killer. He continued – "Police are in the area, asking questions; we should find out who the victim is shortly and why she was in the field."

Alex had read a file on his computer and related his findings to his junior detective – "Regarding these other two cases, Amy Lewis and Jane Hughes, they didn't appear to know each other or have any links through friends or family. As for the other suspects in the area, well, Paul White and Stuart Wilson or 'Half digit' – they have alibis… there's Flora but it's unlikely she could have done any of these killings, she's far too frail and she was at the dentist on the afternoon Amy was killed, it's been checked out. All the other acquaintances of Amy and Jane had solid alibis as well."

He searched for the list of all the blue estate cars in the

area, which had been sent to his computer.

"You do realize, you are on this list as you own a blue estate car and live in the area we are investigating," Alex remarked turning to face his colleague Sam.

"Yes, I knew my car would come up in the search but at that time in the morning when the murder took place at the pub; I was still in bed, alone, so I have no concrete alibi," Sam replied, looking apprehensive.

"You will have to be treated like everyone else, are you willing to have your car searched without a warrant?" Alex asked.

"Of course! I want to be eliminated from all suspicions as soon as possible, so we can continue with this investigation and find this killer!" Sam exclaimed.

Alex was pleased. "I'll arrange for it to be done immediately. Our next interview is with Paul White's previous landlord, I believe he is back from his holidays, so we shall pay him a visit, see what he has to say for himself."

A police officer rushed into the room through the open door. "I think we have a description of the killer, Sir."

Both detectives looked up in surprise.

"Ada Shelton, an elderly lady, had a male visitor last night around 10 pm. She described the man as being about 6 feet tall, white, probably in his 30s, she said she couldn't see his full face as his hood was partly covering it. She didn't see the colour of his hair either. She did say, he was clean shaven and wearing black clothing. Ada wouldn't let him in her cottage. The man claimed his car had broken down; he had pointed towards the road where the lay-by is situated. He told her his mobile phone had no charge and asked if he could use her telephone to call for help; she told the interviewing officer, the man was very polite." The two detectives looked at each other. The police officer continued – "She told the man to go away or she would phone the police; she was terrified after the other murders and was very suspicious of him."

"Did she hear anything, like screams or shouting?" asked DCI Alex Crawford.

"She heard nothing, she had immediately rung a friend but as the man had walked away, they decided not to report it," the police officer replied.

"I'll get the description out together with the blue estate car, to the media, in case they are connected," DCI Crawford replied. "Well, we can rule out Paul White – he has a beard – but Stuart Wilson is over six feet tall and his red hair would have been hidden by the black hood."

"Strange that he keeps popping up," DI Sam Johnson groaned in dismay.

The two detectives arrived at Jeff Thompson's detached house. He was Paul White's former landlord; Amy had made a good case against him in the small claims court, some time ago. The detectives walked up the narrow path between the drive and the lawn; the grass was burnt brown, the dry hardened soil had cracked due to the lack of rain and the sweltering heatwave. A Range Rover was parked on the driveway, which suggested Jeff was not the killer of the second murder at the pub, where a blue estate car was seen at the time of the killing. Jeff saw them arriving and opened the door before they had time to knock.

"What do you want?" Jeff asked abruptly. The detectives introduced themselves and asked him if they could come in to ask a few questions. Reluctantly he showed the detectives into the lounge where a woman in her 50s was sat knitting a baby's matinee coat.

"It's a DCI and a DI, they want to ask a few questions," Jeff told his wife, who looked up from her knitting and politely asked them to take a seat.

"We believe you know Amy Lewis who was murdered on the 18th August," DCI Crawford began.

"I didn't really know her, she was helping Paul White make a case against me. I've never met her, I don't even know what she looks like," Jeff indignantly replied.

"But you will know her address from the documents sent to the court which you would have received a copy of," the senior detective remarked.

"So, are you implying I killed her?" he sternly replied, as his wife gasped in shock.

The DCI calmly answered – "We are trying to eliminate you from our inquiries, these questions have to be asked. Did you ever go to her property?"

"No, I did not," Jeff answered, becoming more agitated.

"Do you own the vehicle on the driveway or any other vehicle?" Jeff was asked.

"I only own the Range Rover on the driveway; my wife

doesn't drive," he answered abruptly.

"Where were you both on the afternoon of Tuesday 18th August?" DCI Crawford queried.

The couple looked at each other trying to remember where they were. "Ah, we were both at our daughter's house, we were helping to move furniture into her new home," replied Jeff's wife, relieved they had a concrete alibi.

"Yes, that's right, we were moving furniture with our daughter at her place," Jeff replied confidently.

"What is your daughter's name and phone number to verify this, so we can eliminate you from our inquiries?" DI Johnson asked. The alibi was checked out and was found to be correct. The detectives left, they hadn't liked the man; however, he was no longer a suspect.

"We are stalling with these murders, suspect after suspect are being cleared. We will go back to that list of blue estate cars and see if any of the owners are around six feet in height," Alex suggested.

They arrived back at the police station to find that Sam's blue estate car had been thoroughly checked over and no incriminating evidence had been found: Sam was in the clear.

Reports were starting to pour in, to confirm there was no suspicious DNA found at the pub, where Jane Hughes was murdered or even in the carpet that had been vacuumed for evidence of hair and different fibres. No fingerprints were found on the shattered bottle either. The same with the murder weapon – the door stopper, in

Amy's greenhouse.

"The killers must have been wearing gloves, you wouldn't normally be wearing gloves in this heat, so it was all premeditated," Alex stated later.

****

"Hey, look, Alf, there's a newspaper article here from the police, it's asking the general public to report anyone they have seen, who is about six feet in height, white male, clean shaven with a blue estate car in this area! That's our neighbour – it's Gordon's description!" a local elderly woman declared.

"Why do the police want to know that for?" her husband asked becoming more curious.

The elderly woman looked up from the local newspaper and replied, "Well, they wish to eliminate these men from their inquiries, a blue estate car was seen near to the crime scene, at the time of that pub murder in Blackendale, you remember."

"I always thought there was something fishy about Gordon, 'im and his wife kept themselves too much to themselves," her husband replied in a grumpy tone of voice.

"He says he's married but I'm not sure about that," added his suspicious wife.

The man struggled out of his armchair and walked with his zimmer frame to the telephone. "I'll ring the police and let them know about Gordon and his blue estate car."

The policeman who received the call was very interested and took down as many details as he could.

A check was completed on this neighbour, Gordon; it appeared he was not married and, interestingly, he had a police record for assaulting a man. The detectives soon arrived at Gordon's front door. It was a Sunday, so they were hoping he would be at home.

The tall slim, blond male in his 30s answered the front door to his small cottage. The Detective Chief Inspector introduced both of them. The detectives noticed Gordon's very distinguishing features – a long pointed nose and sunken eyes.

"We are in the area questioning people to eliminate them from our inquiries, regarding the three recent murders. May we come in to ask you a few questions?" asked the DCI.

"Yes, you had better come in," Gordon replied; he didn't want the nosey neighbours seeing the detectives on his doorstep. He led them into a small lounge with an empty wood burning stove in an inglenook fireplace; they all took a seat.

"We saw a blue estate car on your drive – does it belong to you?" asked DCI Crawford.

"Yes, it does," Gordon replied, surprised they were interested in his car.

"Where were you on Wednesday 19th August, between five am and seven am?"

Gordon thought for a second and stated, "I was in bed!"

"Can anyone verify that?" Gordon was asked.

"No, I was alone, my wife was away at the time," Gordon informed them.

"Who are you married to?" queried the DCI.

"Tara, that's her nickname, her real name is Gabrielle; she is still away at her friend's house but will be returning this afternoon."

Alex noticed a photo of a couple in a frame, it was stood on a small side table. The woman looked strikingly similar in features, she had a similarly pointed nose and sunken eyes like Gordon.

"Is this your wife," he asked pointing to the photograph.

"Yes, it's a photo of both of us, taken last year on our holidays," Gordon replied, casting his eyes down to the carpet; he didn't like the detectives asking questions about Tara.

"Records show you are not married," the DCI suddenly announced.

Instantly, Gordon looked up – he was very surprised that they had checked up about him. "Well, I may as well tell you as you will find out anyway, Tara is my sister."

The two detectives glanced at each other and wondered why he had told them he was married and his neighbours as well.

"Are you willing to have your car searched to eliminate you from our inquiries?" one of the detectives asked.

Gordon was surprised; however, he quickly answered

– "Of course, you don't need a warrant, I've done nothing wrong."

The detectives searched the car and found traces of blood.

The forensic team was called out; the car was searched for any more blood and other incriminating evidence like fibres and hair. The tiny speck of blood on the driver's seat was swabbed and taken for evidence; Gordon was informed about it.

"I did have a nose bleed one day, so it will be my own blood, I'm sure of that," Gordon explained quite innocently.

"We wish to search your house," DCI Crawford replied in a stern voice. Gordon was a suspect now; he had already lied about his marital status – he owned a blue estate car, he lived in the area being investigated, and had a police record for an assault; he was also about six feet in height and was clean shaven. He fitted the killer's profile perfectly; the police thought they could have the real murderer.

"Hey now, hang on, I've done nothing wrong!" Gordon protested; he was becoming uneasy.

"We can obtain a search warrant, if necessary," DI Johnson informed him.

Gordon relented. "That won't be necessary, feel free to search my home."

It was a two bedroomed cottage; two up two down with a bathroom extension downstairs. The smaller bedroom was used as an office. In the main bedroom was a double bed. The detectives glanced at each other; they realized that incest was going on here as Gordon had told them he was living with his sister. The wardrobes were thoroughly searched, black trousers and a black hooded jacket were found, both items were placed in an evidence bag and taken for forensic analysis. Gordon was bought to the police station for further questioning.

The detective quizzed him. "You say you are living with your sister and there is only one bed in your home, so where do you sleep?"

Gordon looked embarrassed that their guilty secret had been exposed. "I may as well come clean, you'll find out anyway, Tara is my twin sister, we have always been very close growing up." He shuffled uncomfortably in his chair. His blue eyes were wide in their sunken eye sockets; fear was gripping him. He continued – "When we moved to the cottage from London we decided to pretend to be married so as not to cause any suspicion."

"You do realize, The Sexual Offence Act of 2003 makes it illegal to have sex with a sibling," DCI Crawford informed him.

Gordon lowered his eyes in shame.

"When we started getting close at about 14 years of age, we didn't know that, we found comfort with each other as our parents were violent towards us, I would often try to protect my twin."

Alex felt pity towards the twins; but the law was the law, he knew the judge would be lenient with them. He knew deep down that Gordon wasn't the killer, he wouldn't commit murder with the chance of being caught and sent to prison. Gordon loved his sister and would want to be with her to protect her.

"You are on record for an assault…" The detective was quickly interrupted by Gordon.

"I can explain that! Tara was being pestered by a man, he was trying to kiss her against her will, I intervened."

"We will have to charge you both for incest," DCI Crawford announced. Gordon nodded realizing everyone would know about their secret relationship, they would be open to sordid rumours and gossip, yet to him, it was a loving relationship but he knew people wouldn't understand what they had suffered at the hands of their parents. *How could he protect his sister now?* he thought to himself; she was everything to him!

After the interview, the detectives discussed the case in their office.

"We'll keep him in custody until the identity of the DNA profile from the speck of blood taken from his car is determined and Gordon's clothing is checked out for blood splatter, hair, and fibres."

"Gordon probably wouldn't have ever been caught for incest had it not been for this murder inquiry, it's like I said before windows open on people's secret lives when we start investigating a crime," Sam added.

A police officer knocked on the office door and walked in. "Here is the completed file on Amy's dating partners."

The file was read by both of the detectives. Police officers had been to each of the suspect's homes and had interviewed them.

"It looks like they all had solid alibis for the afternoon Amy was killed. Apart from Tony Davies, the one Amy called 'the idiot' for pestering her with his amorous phone calls. We'll interview him and see what he has to say," Alex remarked.

Another police officer rushed in. "The woman in the field is Vera Williams, she would have been out walking her dog – taking a short cut back along the footpath to go home," he hurriedly announced. "The dog was found this morning, not far away under a hedge, it was badly injured and was taken to the local vets."

"That explains the large stones in the road, the killer must have been throwing them at the dog and managed to injure it, he probably did that so he could get back to his car without being attacked," Alex assumed. The puzzling pieces were slowly beginning to fit together.

****

Once the news got out about Vera's murder and that her Jack Russell terrier, Max, had been injured; the whole community was in extreme shock and very anxious. Neighbours were going out in twos and threes and only when it was absolutely necessary. Once the school term started, children were collected from school; they were not allowed to walk or bike home.

A group of people was gathered outside the village shop in Raystone; they could sense the tension in each other's voices.

"Poor Vera, I was only talking to her the other day. She was convinced with her large size and having a dog by her side that she would never be a target for the killer; how wrong she was," the tall woman with heavy makeup on her face, remarked. Spots of rain were beginning to fall from the grey sky but no one noticed, they were so totally absorbed in their conversation.

A small elderly woman, looking wide eyed with fear began to speak. "No one's safe, three murders in such a short time, it's unheard of around these parts. I can't sleep at night, living alone as I do. Every creak and noise gets me thinking, is the killer breaking into my house!"

"I know the feeling, I'm like that," uttered another. The spots of rain turned to a downpour and they all rushed into the small shop for shelter.

"There'll be a post-mortem no doubt and an inquest, it will be a bit before the funeral, Vera's son Jack will have to arrange all that," continued the elderly lady.

"Poor Ada, she's really shaken up, it could have been her! Thank goodness she had the sense to tell that man to go away. It's a pity she hadn't reported it straight away, Vera may have been saved."

"I doubt it, it would have taken about 20 minutes for

the police to arrive and they would have gone to Ada's cottage to question her first. That's if they would have even bothered to investigate, as the man was polite and moved on quietly when Ada wouldn't let him in; he may have not even been the murderer! Anyway, the murder would have already been committed by the time the police would have arrived."

Ada was terribly distressed about the murder in the field next door to her cottage. She couldn't help thinking that if she had let the man into her house to use her telephone, she may have been his victim rather than Vera. She felt guilty in a way, that Vera had been killed and not her. She had ordered some flowers and, with a friend, she laid them near the stone stile close to her house and silently whispered a little prayer for Vera and her faithful dog Max. Other villagers had left flowers in the lay-by near the wooden stile across the field from Ada. The whole village was again in mourning.

Dangerous Action

Josie and Paul had sheltered in the wooden shed at Amy's property when the downpour had started. They had gone to Amy's property to spend their Sunday afternoon gathering produce from the garden and to tidy up. Paul had dug over a plot while Josie had done some hoeing around the cabbages and leeks.

"I love it here, it's so peaceful and I love the garden," Josie remarked in a soft voice. "Listen to those beautiful birds chirping, it's heaven here."

"I love it here too, I've always loved this place, it's like home to me. It's a pity we can't rent it and come and live here," Paul answered enthusiastically. His eyes were shining with his unrealistic thoughts.

"I doubt we could afford the rent, it's a big place," Josie murmured with sadness in her eyes. Paul wrapped his tanned, muscular arms around her slender neck and drew her closer to him.

"At least I have you, that's all that matters." He lowered his head to kiss her lips. Josie lovingly wrapped her arms around his waist. They cuddled for a while, listening to the rain pattering on the shed roof. The shower passed over and they were able to gather up their bowls and basket full of produce and finish for the day.

While they were walking towards the car parked on the road, they heard a hen laying an egg, high pitched squawking could be heard coming from the wooden hen house.

"Poor thing, she sounds in agony," Josie uttered in sympathy.

"A bit like childbirth I suppose," replied Paul amused at her observations.

They arrived home and unpacked and put away the produce – potatoes, onions, salad things, soft fruits, and pea pods; they left some out for their tea.

"Let's have a nap before tea," Paul suggested. His eyes were sparkling, his expression and grin signalled to Josie he desired to make love to her. Her blue eyes twinkled with delight at the thought. They quickly undressed in the bedroom and stood naked across from each other; they lovingly stared at each other's beautiful disrobed tanned bodies. Paul admired her slim frame and her firm breasts and lovely flowing blonde hair draping around her shoulders. He advanced towards her and held her close to his warm nude figure. Their moist lips met, love gently rushed into their veins, their hearts beat in rhythm increasing in speed as the adrenalin surged through their bodies. They cuddled on the top of the bed covers and gently rolled until Paul was lying on top of her; he was breathing with a deep passion for her. The positive loving vibes created a warm glow on Josie's cheeks. Her heart began to pound with excitement and sheer ecstasy as the climax was reached. Paul rolled off her, they were perspiring from the heat and exertion. They lay silent, lingering in the thoughts of love; slowly they both slipped into a peaceful slumber.

Eventually, they awoke when a dog started barking. They dressed while chatting about Amy's garden and the work they still had to do.

Josie started making the tea – she chopped up the onions and beef for a casserole. "How do you get the blood off a chopping board?" she asked, not expecting an answer.

"Do you have any baking powder?" asked Paul, eager to show off his knowledge.

Josie looked in the cupboard and found the small cylindrical plastic container. "Yep, here it is."

Paul rubbed a teaspoonful of the powder into the chopping board where the stains had penetrated into the wood fibres, then he rubbed in a few drops of water. He allowed it to stand, to do its work then scrubbed it with the washing up brush. Finally, he washed the board under the running tap.

"There, no stains, look!" he announced gleefully.

"Where did you learn that trick?" an amused

Josie asked.

"Amy taught me, she knew all the old ways of doing things," Paul replied, grinning from ear to ear.

The following day they were both at work. Josie drove to her dress shop – 'Josie's Boutique' situated on the high street, in the town. Her young shop assistant was waiting at the back door to be let in, to start her day's work. They exchanged news while in the kitchen area at the back of the shop and began their daily routine; they worked well as a team.

The shop had two rows of clothes rails down the centre of the large room, fashionable dresses, skirts, shorts, and blouses of all shapes, colours, and sizes hung limp on their hangers. There were shelves fitted all around the room packed with light summer cardigans, swimwear, lingerie, and casually styled handbags. At one end, near the main door to the shop, stood a counter with voguish costume jewellery displayed on ornamental trees painted in gold. Silky scarves hung over a rail making a colourful feature near the counter. The shop window displayed a beachwear theme with mannequins wearing vibrant coloured swimming costumes with floaty beach sarongs tied around their waists. Huge floppy hats adorned their heads, mirrored sunglasses covered their soulless eyes.

Josie unlocked the glass door to the shop and turned the closed sign to open. She began to think about Paul; she often thought about him when she was working in the shop. He was beginning to be constantly on her mind now they were going to be married; she couldn't wait to have a family with him, she was tremendously happy. Josie would excitedly chat with her assistant about the plans they had made for the wedding while drinking their coffee at break time. That day, Josie also discussed with her assistant about changing the window design to an early autumn theme.

Paul was the same, he thought about Josie all the time at work too; he thought about the many times they had made love, the romps they'd had in Amy's garden. He too was looking forward to becoming her husband and having children together, he thought he would make a wonderful dad. He enjoyed his job as being a mechanic, he liked this hands-on work; he could never be cooped up in a small office, sat at a desk all day. Paul's boss was treating him with a lot more respect now, after the incident of the theft. Thank goodness his son had owned up or he could have lost his job or worse.

When Paul and Josie arrived home from work that evening almost at the exact same time as each other, they found a large brown envelope lying on the mat behind the front door.

"It's addressed to you," Josie remarked, curious as to what it contained.

Paul took it from her hand, he had no idea what it could be. He quickly ripped the envelope open; Josie looked on curious to know the news. Paul carefully read the letter looking confused at first then a very excited, broad grin appeared on his sunburnt face; he glanced at Josie.

Josie seeing his excitement cried out, "What is it, what is it, don't keep me in suspense!"

Paul flicked back his long fringe and eagerly replied "Dear old Amy has left the house and garden to me!" he shrieked with absolute delight; he excitedly grabbed hold of Josie and was madly dancing around the furniture in the room.

Josie's vivacious laugh rang out, the news was sheer happiness. The cat walked into the room wondering what all the fuss was about; she stared at their playful antics.

"Gosh, it's like all my birthdays, all my Christmases and all my paydays are rolled into one big happy day!" cried Paul. He couldn't stop grinning, he read the letter over and over again, to make sure he had understood it correctly.

"I'll put my property up for sale, we could move there immediately," Josie eagerly declared, laughing out loud; it was her dream come true as well.

"Hold on, probate and registry and all that have to be completed first before I get the keys, but what a wonderful surprise, I never knew!" He couldn't stop grinning and occasionally howled with laughter, his fantasy of owning the property he loved so much had finally come true, it all seemed unreal like a fairy tale.

****

The two detectives were driving towards Tony Davies' mobile home on a residential caravan park, which was situated on the outskirts of the town. They drove past a small grocery shop and passed rows of mobile homes with neat little gardens full of pots containing pretty, scented flowers in bloom. It was a bright sunny day, not a cloud in the sky; the white picket fences around some of the gardens gleamed in the glaring sunshine.

DI Sam Johnson knocked on the door of the light green painted mobile home, and a grey-haired man opened the door. The detectives introduced themselves and he cheerfully invited them inside. They noticed he had a prosthetic right leg when he walked in front of them to show them into the lounge.

The room was fitted with comfy sofas; the fireplace was partly jutting out into the room making a partial partition with the dining area. A wide flat screen television hung over the fireplace.

"We believe you knew Amy Lewis," began one of the detectives. "We bring the sad news that she has been murdered."

"I saw it on the local news and in the newspaper; I was absolutely gutted. Poor old dear, I loved her to bits you know, I would have married her and would have loved her to the day I died," the grey-haired man replied. He was gazing into the distance, deep in thought of the happy times he had spent with Amy. He had no idea it wasn't mutual; he would have been very upset to learn Amy had referred to him as 'the idiot'. He was the romantic type, offering flowers, presents, and romantic poems to woo his lady friends.

"We are asking everyone who knew Amy – where were you on 18th August in the afternoon?" asked DCI Alex Crawford. He scrutinized the man's facial expression to see if he was telling any lies.

"I was here!" Tony Davies exclaimed, wiping away a tear from his eye with his thin, wrinkly fingers.

"Can anyone vouch for that?" the detective asked.

"I don't know, it depends if one of my neighbours saw me about or noticed my car parked outside," the man replied, looking shocked that he appeared to be a suspect.

"Your car isn't there at the moment," observed the DI.

"It's in the garage for its MOT, I'll be collecting it later," Tony Davies announced. He was beginning to feel uncomfortable with these questions.

"What colour and make of car is it?" asked the DCI.

Tony replied giving a laborious poetic description of his car which he referred to as 'his baby'. The detectives were satisfied it wasn't the blue estate car seen near the pub on the morning of Jane Hughes' murder. The detectives left, much to the relief of Tony.

They began to question his neighbours nearby about the afternoon of 18th August and if they had seen Tony Davies or his car on his drive.

"What day was that?" asked one individual, leaning on his walking stick. He was wearing a white Panama hat to shade his eyes from the bright sunlight. His face was spotted with dark discolorations and deep wrinkles.

"Tuesday," came the reply. The elderly man turned to his wife who was sat in a rocking chair on the veranda; she was wearing a straw sunhat to shade her eyes. She wore a long flowing, purple flowered skirt to protect her legs from the burning sun.

"Didn't I ask Tony Davies if he would lend me an electric drill when we drove past his place to go to the doctor's appointment, was that Monday or Tuesday, dear?"

"Yes, you did ask him, you'd better remember to return it! I can't remember the date; I'll have to check the calendar." The large old woman struggled out of her rocking chair and waddled into her mobile home. She reappeared holding her picture calendar.

"Yes, dear, your doctor's appointment was definitely Tuesday at three pm." She handed the calendar to the detective for him to check the date and time.

"Thank you for your help, we can now eliminate Tony Davies from our inquiries," the lead detective informed them.

At the police station, the detectives were in a sombre mood.

"The cases are going cold, we have 50 plus officers working on these cases and no clues can be found," Alex remarked. He was extremely concerned that the killers were still on the loose and could kill again. "Our only suspect, Gordon, the twin, is now cleared regarding the speck of blood in his car; it was his own, probably from his nose bleed, like he told us. We have nothing on him apart from his incest with his twin sister. That will be dealt with in the courts, it's out of our hands now."

His colleague Sam sighed. "Let's go through all the notes again and see if we can spot something we've missed." He picked up a file. "We can put this file aside, the men Amy dated – Len Cartwright, looking for a mummy wife." The detective chuckled. "Adrian Jackson was supposed to be after Amy's money and Ben Walton, the sex maniac, they've all got concrete alibis, so has Tony Davies the amorous telephone caller we've just visited."

"Jeff Thompson, Paul White's landlord, was moving furniture at the time of Amy's murder, Flora was at the dentist and Paul White was with his girlfriend. The vending machine man; well, I'm still suspicious of him but the time of death was too early, he was still in that meeting. I wonder if the forensic pathologist could have been wrong about the time of death?" questioned the senior detective; he began stroking his chin in deep thought.

"Stuart Wilson does appear to be popping up a few times and he has the links to the victims owning the vending machines," Sam added. After much thought, he continued. "Although, Vera Williams, murdered in that field, she hadn't got anything to do with vending machines, had she?"

"This report says Vera used to own a betting shop before she retired, and guess what – she had gaming vending machines ordered from Stuart Wilson, our half fingered man. I'll have him interviewed again, see if he has a rock-solid alibi for the time of Vera's death. Is it a coincidence or is he killing off all his previous customers that gave him grief perhaps?" Alex quizzed.

"Time will tell, I have my suspicions of him too. Don't forget the dopey lodger on our list, who did a moonlight flit; he was sunbathing on a beach with his girlfriend at the time of Amy's murder, I think his alibi is quite solid though. If it's not Stuart Wilson; it's looking more like an opportunist from outside the area," Sam suggested.

"No, I disagree. Amy lived down a road out of the way, only a local would know about it. The woman murdered in the field was another unknown footpath if you weren't local. No, we are missing something here." The two detectives continued 'throwing' ideas around until it was time to leave.

"Do you fancy a pint, Sam?"

"No, not tonight, I've got a date with the lovely Annette," Sam replied with a beaming grin.

"Oh yes, how did the other night go?" probed Alex.

"I took her for a meal at the new restaurant in town; we are getting along great!" Sam enthusiastically answered.

"Well done, you, I'm glad you have found a lovely woman." Alex was genuinely pleased; he wanted his friend and colleague to have the opportunity to settle down with a suitable partner.

"I know you set it up with your scheming wife, Verona, at the barbecue, you were both wanting Annette and me to meet." Sam laughed with a glint in his eye. Alex laughed with him, pleased he was happy with the outcome.

When Alex, arrived home, he told Verona their match-making had worked, and she was so pleased.

"It's about time Sam got himself a decent woman, I never liked any of his other girlfriends and they never seemed to last. Are you any nearer to catching these killers?" asked his concerned wife.

"No, it's so frustrating, just when we think we have a good lead it rapidly becomes obvious it's not. How are the locals coping?" Alex asked; he was concerned for the communities involved.

"There is a tremendous amount of fear out there, most people are remaining indoors in this sweltering heat, too afraid to even sunbathe in their own gardens. When word got out about Vera Williams had been brutally murdered and her dog savagely injured, dog walkers began walking out in groups!"

"I hope we can catch the killers soon; I feel totally responsible for all the women who have been murdered, their lives cut short. It's such a tragedy," Alex sadly replied; he was full of an overwhelming sense of duty to the communities to bring these killers to justice.

The following morning, while Alex was in his office, a young policewoman handed him a letter. "It's just arrived in the post, it was unusual so I thought you should see it first."

He opened the scrawling handwritten brown envelope carefully, to prevent any of his fingerprints being left on the item. It was addressed to 'The Police Station, Longtown'. Inside he found a note; it had been typed on a computer keyboard and printed out. It was all in capital letters.

TO THE POLICE

SO YOU HAVEN'T FIGURED IT ALL OUT YET! HA HA I'M GONNA DO IT AGAIN!

It was like being punched in the gut, the writer of the note was mocking the police and taunting them. Sam entered the room just at that moment.

"Take a look at this, it arrived in the mail, just now." Sam took the note using his handkerchief and read it.

"It's a hoax!" he exclaimed and threw the note onto the desk in disgust.

"I feel the same, if it was the real killer, he would have told us an important detail about the murders that had not been released to the general public; like he used a bottle for the pub murder or a stone for the field murder. If it was Amy's killer, he would have mentioned the brass door stopper. He would have definitely done that to gloat... there are some sick bastards about. The envelope is handwritten not like the note, we'll give them to forensics and see if the sender was stupid enough to have left his fingerprints or DNA on them. I'll get this handwriting to the media, see if anyone recognizes it."

Sam was eager to get home that night, to shower and change for another date. He phoned Annette to say he would meet her at the pub on the corner of Angel Lane at eight pm and they could decide from there where to go. He thought she was really beautiful and smart too, an ideal partner for him. He had high hopes of a long-term relationship with her. She wasn't like the other girls he had been out with, most of those casual girlfriends had slept around and were not interested in settling down to a committed relationship.

****

"Where could she be?" a distressed mother was frantically asking her worried husband.

Their feisty 16 year old daughter, Lizzie, had left the house after a blazing row with her parents. The row was over Lizzie being invited to stay with a mixed group of 16 year old friends at a remote holiday cottage in the Lake District. Her parents had disapproved of the plan when they heard there wouldn't be any parents there to supervise them. Lizzie had worked herself into a hot temper and had been screaming at them, saying they didn't trust her; she was an adult now and could look after herself. Her parents tried in vain to explain but Lizzie was adamant; she stormed out of the house in a rage. Her father had tried to run after her, but Lizzie was a lot younger and fitter than he was and she had managed to escape. Lizzie was in no mood for reasoning.

Worried sick that a serial killer was still on the loose,

her parents had rung around all her friends to see if she had gone to one of their houses; they in turn frantically rang everyone they knew – Lizzie was nowhere to be found. After an hour of searching, both her parents were extremely anxious and worried sick at the lack of news; they decided to call the police. The call was taken very seriously as a murderer was still on the loose in the area. A policewoman immediately called at the house to obtain further details.

"She has just turned 16, she thinks she's invincible as they all do at that age, I'm so frightened she may have been murdered," the mother told the police officer and began to sob uncontrollably.

Lizzie's father spoke in a troubled voice. "It's all about the row we had with her. We wouldn't allow her to go to the Lake District with her friends, we felt she was too young to be able to control a situation if things got out of hand, you know, getting drunk and the boys taking advantage, that sort of thing. We told her she wasn't going and that was that. She was very angry and ran out of the house, I ran after her but I couldn't keep up; she just disappeared. We've rung everyone we could think of, she's not turned up anywhere!"

"Let me have the details of what she was wearing and have you a recent photo of her?" asked the policewoman. The mother lifted up a school photo from the mantelpiece and removed the photo out of its silver frame. She had tears in her eyes as she handed the large photo to the policewoman. The mother didn't know if she would ever see her daughter again. Lizzie had an abundance of long wavy red hair; she had a beautiful charismatic smile and rosy cheeks.

"She's a good looking girl, we will do our utmost to find her, don't you worry. Now, we need her date of birth, height, weight..." The words became blurred as the distraught mother was in deep shock and distress and could only think of her beloved daughter out there alone, with a killer on the loose. The father answered the questions as best he could.

An alert had immediately gone out on the parents' first phone call, to the police on duty; these other details were also relayed to every police officer in the area. It was a race against time to find her before the killer found her and made her his next victim.

Lizzie had found a place to sob her heart out in a park nearby, she had curled up on a park bench, her arms around her knees, her head bowed. She was still extremely angry; she hated her parents. She was 16 now – how dare they stop her enjoying herself with her friends. Her mum and dad were always interfering in her life, she just wanted to do her own thing and enjoy life. She knew she could look after herself, she didn't need adults to chaperone her! Tears were streaming down her face; she felt very frustrated and very irate indeed.

Suddenly, she heard a car. She looked up, thinking her parents had found her. Instead, she saw a blue estate car travelling on the road nearby; the driver had seen her! It flashed through her mind that the police were interested in a blue estate car seen near to the pub murder! Her heart sank with the awful realization that she wasn't safe outside alone. Sheer terror gripped her very core.

The blue estate car pulled up on the roadside. Lizzie's heart rate was starting to wildly race with fear and dread. She swiftly lurched into action and started to run as fast as her legs could carry her.

The tall man had spotted the girl, he knew her, he had recognized her flowing red wavy hair and had noticed that she was vulnerable and completely alone. He speedily jumped out of his car, he called out, "Lizzie, stop, stop!" He began to race after her. Lizzie's hearing had become so acute with the terror gripping her body, she could hear every footstep behind her, coming closer and closer.

She clumsily tripped and fell over some stones, she struggled to her feet and started to run as fast as she could again. The man was gaining on her with his lengthy strides. Her mind was in overdrive, *is he the killer? Am I going to die? Who is he?* Words were flashing through her mind – *what should I do? I'll never outrun him.* She hurriedly decided to quickly dart and hide behind thick bushes, in the undergrowth; she lay there very still, hardly daring to breathe. Her chest was still heaving as she was out of breath.

She heard him call out – "Lizzie, Lizzie, your parents are worried sick, let me take you home."

It was a trick, she knew it, she lay as still as she could.

Straining her ears in the direction the man was coming towards her. Every minute that passed, seemed to be like an hour as she listened intently. She heard his footsteps coming closer and closer; she hardly dared to breathe; he walked quite near to her and stopped. Her body was perfectly still, thankfully he didn't appear to see or hear her, not even her pounding heart, that filled her head with the terrifying thumping noise.

She lay there motionless, for ages, her bare right leg was getting nettled, but she didn't dare move an inch, she suffered the pain and the itching in total silence. She was aware something was crawling over her other leg, and normally she would have screamed out in fright; instead, she creased her eyes shut and held her breath until the creepy crawly had gone. All her five senses were intensely sharp due to the acute fear gripping her; she strained her ears listening for every sound. Paranoid thoughts wandered and weaved through her distraught mind, as she tried to make up her mind what to do. She could smell the strong odour from the grass, soil, and the weeds surrounding her; her fearful eyes strained to see in the darkness.

Suddenly, she could feel a spider walking onto her hand, a big blob of a body and massive long legs; she was petrified of spiders. She flicked her hand violently to knock the spider off, desperately trying not to scream.

She felt so sick and afraid, *was this the place she would be murdered and left there to rot?* she thought to herself. If only she was safe at her comfortable home.

The air was cooling rapidly; she only had a top with straps and shorts on, goosebumps were appearing on her arms; she shuddered in the chilly night air. She would have to cope with the cold – her life was at stake.

It was ages before she plucked up the courage to look farther afield. She couldn't see the tall man anywhere in the darkness. She didn't know whether to start running again or just remain hidden and wait. *Was he there waiting for her to surface?* These thoughts made her heart begin to thump so violently; she could feel it in her throat. She had never been so frightened in all her life. She began to feel remorse at screaming at her caring parents, she just longed to be in their loving arms, feeling secure and happy again.

It could have been an hour before she plucked up the courage to start running again, the silence and darkness sent shudders down her spine; she hoped she wasn't running in the direction of the killer. She ran out of the wooded area as fast as she could. She came to a shrubbery area then into an open area with paths, benches, and lawns. She felt vulnerable in the open space, but it was the only way to the main gates and back to her house. She saw a light coming towards her, she panicked, *the killer had gone back to the car for a torch,* she thought to herself. She started seeing lots of lights coming towards her, so she stopped, frozen to the spot – *was she imagining all this? I can't run the other way, it's where the killer's car is, what should I do?* She was thinking in extreme panic. The clearing where she stood had little cover; panic-stricken she ran to the only tree in the vicinity and hid behind it, breathing heavily.

"Lizzie, Lizzie it's the police, we have your parents here!" a loud voice called out on seeing movement in the distance.

It's a trick, it's a trick, she thought to herself over and over again, still terrified of every person in case they were the killer. She was in deep emotional distress and petrified for her life. She trusted no one.

"Lizzie, Lizzie don't be afraid, it's your dad, we are not angry with you, please show yourself, we want to take you home, we love you, please come home," Lizzie's father desperately called out, hoping and praying the movement they had seen in the distance was their daughter.

Lizzie recognized her father's pleading voice and ran out; she was in floods of tears of relief. She was safe at last and would never question her parents' concerns ever again. She knew she had grown up a lot that night and could now see her parents' point of view, instead of focusing on her own selfish needs. The torch lights came nearer as searchers ran towards her.

It was an extremely emotional reunion, even the police and neighbours that had turned out to look for her were holding back their tears. It was a relief they had found her safe and sound apart from a few scrapes, bruises, and nettle stings to her knees and her calf on her leg. Many wondered if they would be finding a corpse with the skull smashed in, so they were extremely happy to see her alive!

Her father saw she was shivering with cold and maybe

in shock. He lovingly placed his warm anorak around her slim shoulders. She felt the heat surrounding her body and was thankful for the feeling of warmth and security.

"I saw the killer! He got out of his blue estate car and ran after me. I hid under a bush and waited until I thought it was safe to run again," she hysterically explained, then she turned to her mother. "Oh, Mum, I'm so sorry, I will never run off like that again. I was so scared," Lizzie cried out. Her mother hugged her, releasing all the pent-up emotions, and burst into floods of tears along with her daughter.

"It was a police detective that spotted you. When he couldn't find you, after you had run away from him; he alerted the police and us. That's when we organized the search; look – all the neighbours turned out!" her father exclaimed, trying to explain to her what had happened. He put his loving arm around her to comfort her.

Lizzie burst into tears again, overwhelmed at the love and care everyone had shown her. She had been so foolish to run off like that, she knew now; it had panicked her loved ones and caused a lot of emotional anguish to everyone. She found out later that it was Sam Johnson, the detective inspector who had tried to help her and she was able to thank him personally and say sorry.

Sam had to explain to his girlfriend that the date they had arranged that night, would have to be postponed. He told her he was searching for a missing girl, that she was in terrible danger as the serial killer was still on the loose. Annette understood perfectly and arranged another day and time.

The staff at the police station grinned and enthusiastically clapped their hands as Sam proudly walked into work the following morning, his broad grin stretched across his face, from ear to ear.

"Congratulations, Sam, on seeing the girl and alerting everyone, Lord knows what could have happened if the killer had seen her first," Alex remarked as he patted Sam on his back.

"I was just doing my duty, like any one of you here would have done," Sam replied modestly.

The two detectives walked into their office and shut the door.

"I hope Annette didn't mind her date being cancelled."

"Not cancelled, postponed – we are going out again," grinned Sam.

"Well, let's get down to business; shall we? I've got a report here, an officer interviewed Stuart Wilson last evening about his whereabouts at the time of Vera Williams' murder in the field. Stuart told the officer he was out with friends that night, so he had plenty of witnesses; they have been contacted and can corroborate his story. So, he's out of the picture again."

"What about the envelope and handwritten note – did forensics work on that last night?" asked Sam, eager to know the outcome.

"Yes, they did and at long last, we have a fingerprint,

it was found on the envelope; they ran it through the database and found a match!"

"Great, who is he?" asked Sam.

"He doesn't live anywhere near this area, he is called Harry Martin, a builder's labourer, he doesn't possess a blue estate car or has ever owned one."

"Was it all just a hoax then?" asked Sam, his voice showing his disappointment.

"It's looking like it; his local police have arrested him and are questioning him, we may know the answers later today," Alex informed him. They were both disheartened with the cases, but thanks to Sam they had saved the girl.

"So, we are back to square one, these cases are going cold," murmured Sam.

A Potential Clue

An unexpected call came into the police station; it was redirected to Alex, the lead detective.

"I only wanted to speak to you," a quiet nervous voice began. "I have some information for you. I'm Stuart Wilson's wife, Jackie." There was a pause.

"Take your time, Jackie, just relax," the detective replied in a calming, soothing voice.

"I must tell you, he, I mean my husband borrows his father's blue estate car from time to time, I thought you should know that," the woman blurted out in a rush, meek tone of voice. She gave the name and address of her father-in-law.

Had Jackie rung with this information to create a path to her freedom? Alex thought to himself.

"Jackie, I'm pleased you have rung me; thank you for your information. Can you remember if Stuart had the blue estate car on the 18th and 19th August?" DCI Alex

Crawford asked; relieved they could now possibly link the vending machine man with the blue car seen at the time of the pub murder.

"I'm very sorry but I can't remember," Jackie replied in a faint voice.

"The morning you told us you were both in bed between five and seven am, have you remembered anything more?" the detective inquired, trying to coax out any more information.

Jackie tried to explain. "Well, when I woke about 7 o'clock, that's when the alarm clock goes off, Stuart was already downstairs, he was already dressed. He could have been out, I don't know, I really don't know."

Alex was patient with Jackie, he knew how scared she must be. "What about the alibi for the night the woman was murdered in the field? Stuart told us he was with a lot of other people – is that correct?"

"Yes, we were at a large party, everyone was drunk, it's possible he could have slipped out unnoticed, I suppose, I don't know." Jackie was starting to have doubts whether she should have rung, she didn't know anything for sure.

"On the 18th August, when Amy Lewis was murdered, did he behave normally when he came home, were his clothes blood stained?"

Jackie was nervous at being questioned. "He has never come home with blood-stained clothes; I can't remember about his behaviour, I'm sorry, I rang because I thought you should know about the blue estate car."

"Thank you for your information, Jackie, I know it has taken a great deal of courage for you to ring me today. If you think of anything else, please ring me immediately." The DCI hoped Jackie would keep in touch – she could have more vital information.

The detective smiled as he replaced the receiver. He informed the local police station of Stuart's father's address – they would have to interview the father. *We need confirmation of the dates when Stuart borrowed his father's car,* he pondered.

****

Paul and Josie had returned to Amy's garden and after completing their jobs, Paul took Josie into the stone outhouse situated at the far corner of the vegetable garden.

"I think it's in here," Paul told her. "Amy has a plastic bin buried in the ground somewhere."

"Why would she have a bin underground?" Josie laughed at such a weird idea.

"It keeps things cool like a fridge; look, there's a paving stone, I bet it's under here." Paul dropped to his knees and eased the stone slab away from the top of the hole. He lifted up the layer of fleece material sitting on top of the bin's lid which was keeping it insulated. He opened the lid by releasing the catches on either side.

"What's in it?" asked Josie peering over his shoulder.

"Bags of dried vegetable seeds, a bag of grain like

barley or something; not much else." He spoke in a disappointed voice.

"Barley! Does she grow her own barley?" Josie chuckled.

"I know she has in the past; she has her own hand mill and grinder, she'd shown them to me, she used to dry the barley grains and grind them up. She sometimes made barley bread!" Paul replaced the bin lid and the insulating material and slid the paving stone back over the hole. An idea struck him. "Hey, let's go and see the inside of the house!"

Josie's eyes lit up with his excitement, she was eager this time to see inside the house, now that they were going to own it.

"Can we go in without permission, do you think?" she asked hesitating.

"No one will know, will they!" Paul replied grinning with a twinkle in his eyes.

Josie grew anxious. "There won't be any blood or anything like that in there, will there?"

"No, the police will have had it all cleaned up for the next owners. I think Flora has also been in to tidy up the kitchen." Paul stretched up his arm, to a ledge in the outhouse to retrieve the key. They walked down the garden path arm in arm, joking and laughing. Paul unlocked the back door and they ventured inside.

The kitchen had been tidied up and everything on the sides had been put away. Josie looked around with a blank expression on her face. They opened the wooden latched door to the pantry.

"Flipping heck, what are these?" asked Josie, picking up a jar of alien looking peas.

Paul laughed. "They are nasturtium seeds, I think they are called; you can eat them, they taste peppery or spicy. They are called the poor man's capers. You can eat the whole plant which also tastes peppery, including the flowers – they taste sweet!"

"Ugh, I don't fancy them," Josie replied, screwing up her face in disgust; she replaced the jar on the shelf. "Gosh, there's everything here," she muttered, reading the labels. "Beetroot, jam, pickled eggs, string beans, dried peas, and dried beans... what's in here?" Josie was lifting up a lid from the glazed pot that stood on the floor.

"It's salted cabbage, it's how they preserved it in the old days. You don't eat it like that, it has to be put in water, for a few days, to get rid of the salt. The water has to be changed a few times."

Josie was fascinated and looked around the large room with the numerous shelves, stacked with glass bottles and jars; all had a neat little hand printed label on them.

She looked up to the white painted ceiling. "What's all these hanging from the ceiling? I know these are onions."

"Dried herbs... sage, mint, and things like that," Paul replied. "She would sprinkle crushed herbs into stews, soups, and over her scrambled eggs and things."

Josie noticed a jar she had missed. "Dried orange peel!" Josie cried out and laughed at the jar on the shelf in front of her.

"Yes, there's lots of ways to use it, like in marinades, infusions, tea, and potpourri for instance," Paul explained enthusiastically.

"I can see she taught you a lot about the old ways." Josie suddenly tripped on the tray of crushed eggshells. "What the dickens did she use those for?"

Paul chuckled to himself. "Well, they are a great source of calcium for the garden or for eating. They can deter slugs because of the sharp edges. You can feed them to the hens as well, there are lots of ways to use them; nothing was wasted with Amy!" Paul explained, giggling.

"You can actually eat eggshells?" Josie thought he was pulling her leg.

"Yes, but you have to bake them in the oven and boil them to get rid of any nasties; they have to be ground up into a powder as well to be able to be eaten." Paul grinned at Josie's surprised look.

Paul showed her another glass jar. "Look, this is apple cider vinegar."

Josie looked at the clear liquid inside the jar with apple cores floating at the top; some had sunk to the bottom.

"It has fantastic healing and cleansing properties. Amy told me it was good for sore throats if you added honey; it also cures bad breath, helps weight loss I believe in small doses, and also makes your hair shine as well and gets rid of dandruff! It can be used in tons of ways, but I've forgotten most of them."

"Wow, you don't need all this expensive stuff from shops then!" Josie exclaimed as she was beginning to realize Amy's old ways weren't so crazy after all.

"That's what Amy used to say, but we have lost the knowledge of the old ways since these big corporations took over. Amy hated their wasteful, polluting plastic bottles for everything and especially the spray plastic bottles." They walked back into the kitchen.

"We will definitely have to have a new kitchen installed, I don't like this old fashioned one," Josie remarked with a frown.

"The equity from your house should just about cover the cost of a modern kitchen," replied Paul, thinking the mortgage would have to be paid off and there wouldn't be much left. They walked by the wooden kitchen table and stools into the cosy sitting room. Paul had his arm cuddling Josie around her waist.

"I love the wood burning stove, but this old decor needs changing in here," Josie uttered as she observed the dingy room.

"We could do that ourselves; a 'lick of paint' will brighten the old place up," Paul suggested.

"Let's see what's upstairs." Josie was full of curiosity to see the rest of her future home. Upstairs were two bedrooms, a box room, and a bathroom.

"This used to be my little bedroom in here," Paul told her, leading her into a plain small room with a bed, wardrobe, and shelves. The window had a fine view overlooking the vegetable garden.

"I can see why you were happy here; later you gave it all up to come and live with me. It's wonderful how it's all worked out though. It's amazing that you are going to come back and live here as the owner. It's a dream come true!" Josie squealed with excitement. "Amy knew what she was doing gifting this place to you; she wanted you to carry on her legacy."

"Yes, I believe you are right! I'll do my utmost to carry on her legacy. It sure is a dream come true all this and the best part is you are going to live here with me as well!" They both laughed, full of happiness and gratitude.

They walked into the box room and could see it was Amy's office. Josie felt she was intruding into Amy's personal life. She turned to walk into Amy's room, and Paul followed her. Flora had made the bed and washed Amy's clothes and put them neatly away in the wardrobe and drawers.

"This is a nice sized room, it feels light and airy with the two sets of windows; we will have this room and sleep in here… it has a good outlook too, over the fields, lake, and the woods," Josie murmured, peering out of one of the windows. Paul was watching Josie intently, he loved her so much; he was excited that she was taking a real interest in the house. He gently pushed her onto the bed, and Josie squealed with surprise.

"No, we can't do it here, not in Amy's bed and someone may come." Josie wasn't feeling confident yet in

Amy's house.

"OK, another time. What do you think then, will you be happy here?" Paul eagerly asked, holding her close to him after she had scrambled off the bed.

"Of course, I'll be happy especially with you at my side." They kissed each other tenderly and warmly hugged each other.

****

The following morning, Alex had received a report on Harry Martin, the builder's labourer. He was a known petty thief, so his fingerprints were recorded on the database. He had been taken in for questioning at his local police station in his own area. The police had questioned him regarding the letter that had been sent to the police. His fingerprint had been discovered on the handwritten envelope, so he was identified.

Harry Martin had never possessed a blue estate car. He had been asked to give a sample of his writing; he was left handed and wrote in a similar fashion to the scrawling handwriting on the envelope. His fingerprints were also taken to check that no mistakes had been made with the information on the database. Both his handwriting and fingerprint were a match with the evidence.

When Harry Martin was confronted with all the evidence, he readily confessed to sending the hoax letter. He had a low IQ and desperately wanted to be famous; no one had ever taken any notice of him until he was in trouble with the police for petty theft. That attention didn't last long and he was eager for more recognition. He wanted to be on the front page of the national newspapers, and on the television and radio. He wanted everyone to know his name. He was enjoying all this latest attention.

The detective saw another lead had met a dead end. He read about the other information he had received about Stuart Wilson's father. He owned a blue estate car but was away in his car on holiday at the time of Amy Lewis' and Jane Hughes' murder, so his son Stuart couldn't have used the car in any of those murders. The detective was feeling discouraged at the lack of evidence. The clock was ticking to his retirement date; he desperately wanted to solve these murders so he could retire on a good note and in peace.

Sam walked in grinning and soon realized his boss wasn't happy.

"Read these," Alex murmured, turning his computer around on his desk. Sam sat down in the chair by the desk and studied the reports.

"Looks like we are back to square one again!" Sam gloomily replied after reading through the information.

Alex replied, "These are probably the most frustrating cases I've ever worked on; I'm determined to solve them and bring these killers to justice before I retire... I forgot to ask, how did your date with Annette go? I saw you walking in here 'grinning like a Cheshire cat'."

"It went well, we plan to go away for a weekend to

the Lake District; can you recommend anywhere?" Sam inquired.

Alex thought for a moment. "My wife should be able to help you out with that."

The phone rang at that instance.

A hurried anxious voice spoke out. "You are needed at Stuart Wilson's house; neighbours have reported a violent row is in progress with him and his wife. I know she will only speak to you, so I thought you should be there."

"Right, I'm on my way." The two detectives hurried out of the office, discussing the phone call.

When they arrived at the Victorian house, they drove up the steep tree-lined driveway and raced to the door. Alex rang the ornate doorbell; there was silence. They couldn't hear any shouting from inside.

A few moments before the detectives had arrived, Stuart Wilson had been angrily shouting at his wife, Jackie. He had suspected her of informing the police that he sometimes borrowed his father's blue estate car – *how else would they know?* he had questioned himself.

His father had rung him at work that morning and told him about the visit from the police. Stuart in a rage had immediately jumped into his car and driven home to confront his wife, Jackie.

He had rushed upstairs in a foul temper, shouting angrily. He saw Jackie rushing onto the landing wondering why Stuart had returned to the house. They met each other at the top of the stairs; an argument ensued. It became more angry and violent, Stuart started punching his wife in the face, Jackie was screaming and crying as he lashed out.

"Stop, stop, you are hurting me." There was no mercy.

The final blow was hard, it knocked Jackie completely off balance and she fell, rolling and tumbling down the stairs. Her head landed on the floor tiles below with a resounding crack. Her whole body had tumbled into a crumpled heap at the foot of the stairway; her ash blonde hair splayed out on the sandstone tiled floor. Stuart ran down the stairs and towered over her.

"Get up, get up," he screamed in an incoherent voice; he kicked her side with his foot. Jackie lay there motionless, and the sudden realization hit Stuart – he knew then he had killed her. He heard the doorbell ring; he waited for a few seconds, thinking it was all over now, and calmly opened the door. The detectives saw the blood on his knuckles and asked to speak to his wife.

Stuart opened the door wide in a sort of daze. The detectives could see Jackie crumpled up with one foot resting on the bottom step. Alex rushed to her side, while Sam detained Stuart Wilson from leaving the premises.

The DCI desperately felt for a pulse. "She's dead!" the detective announced, sickened by her injuries. "How did this happen?" he shouted in a loud voice.

Stuart placidly replied, "She's always tripping and falling, she's fallen downstairs this time. I've just found her; I was about to call the ambulance when you arrived."

The house soon began to fill up with police crime scene

investigators wearing protective clothing.

Nick, the portly pathologist arrived. "Dreadful, shocking, this all is," he murmured, shaking his head from side to side. He knelt down on the cool sandstone tiles to examine the body. "She's hasn't been dead very long, minutes I'd say, not even an hour. I would think she has broken her neck, she has also a nasty laceration to the left eye, there's also massive bruising to the face," the pathologist announced.

Blood spots were found at the top of the stairs on the wall, samples were taken for evidence. The neighbours were interviewed, they all informed the police, the violent row had stopped just seconds before the detectives had arrived at the house.

Stuart Wilson was arrested on suspicion of murder and taken to the police station. On his way there, he was desperately trying to think of an alibi to get himself out of this mess. His concern was for himself not for his dead wife; she was gone now, it was his life that could drastically change. His large hands were swabbed for evidence as it was noticeable that blood had dried in the creases of his knuckles of his right hand. A single eyelash was retrieved from the dried blood. He was asked to remove his clothing as his clothes would be required to be thoroughly examined for blood splatter.

Alex was feeling distraught; if they had arrived earlier, Jackie could still have been alive for them to stop the violent abuse and her death. He was restless, chewed up with emotions for the meek and defenceless woman. She had trusted him enough to ring him about the blue estate car; however, she had put herself in dreadful danger. He felt it was his fault, he should have done more to protect her.

Stuart Wilson was shown into the interview room wearing a garment a police officer had asked him to slip on. He'd been in an interview room before so he knew the routine. He sat on a chair opposite the detectives, at a wooden table. He felt quite confident with a smug grin on his face.

He had told the detectives, "I don't need a solicitor as I've done nothing wrong, I found my wife lying at the bottom of the stairs when I came home for a file; I'd forgotten to take it to work with me that morning."

He denied everything and had an aloof and almost grandiose style attitude about him. He ran his fingers through his distinctive short, red curly hair; his half finger on his right hand was extremely noticeable. Although the detectives detested the man, they had to remain calm and amiable. The interview was eventually terminated, the detectives would wait for the analyst's reports on the crime scene and the results from the forensic pathologist.

****

Paul and Josie arrived at Amy's funeral, they had decided to wear black as Amy was very old fashioned about funeral attire, she would always attend funerals in black. Flora was there with a few of Amy's neighbours and friends; the whole village seemed to have turned out to pay their respects. Many had to stand outside as there was no more room indoors. The two detectives, Alex and Sam, also attended. They were representing the police force.

It was a simple funeral service; Amy had planned it herself to be held at the local crematorium. She didn't want to be buried, *'taking up space on earth'*, she thought it was wasteful. Typically, she didn't want a wooden coffin either, *'an eco-friendly wicker coffin will do for me'* she had told her friend, Flora. There were no flowers, she had insisted on donations instead; she wanted the money to go to the homeless.

Paul and Josie were amazed at the turnout. Paul had been approached to say a few words and he was honoured to do so. He nervously cleared his throat; he spoke about the woman he called 'Mum' and how she had taught him her many skills. He emphasized how happy he was to have been a small part of this wonderful woman's life. He vowed he would carry on the legacy she had left him. It brought tears to Josie's eyes; she was so proud of Paul.

The detectives were looking around the room at the tearful mourners, wondering if her murderer was present, possibly gloating at his evil deed. Amy had insisted she didn't want a wake – *'Why waste money on that, the funeral service will be sufficient,'* she had insisted to Flora when arrangements for her funeral were made.

After the service everyone gathered outside; the

detectives were still on the alert, watching the crowd to see if they could spot anyone behaving abnormally. The neighbours, friends, and villagers behaved genuinely in their grief for this remarkable woman, her life cut short in a most heinous way.

****

The following day, the detectives were receiving information about the pathologist report. Stuart's wife, Jackie Wilson, had multiple bruises to her face, her left eye socket was broken as well as her neck which was the probable cause of her death. There were other injuries to her body that were probably sustained during the fall. Old bruising was also recorded in the report as being significant as it wasn't normal for extensive bruising like this to be present on a body unless they had been in a car accident or something similar.

The eyelash was reported to belong to the deceased. There was a tiny amount of blood splatter on Stuart Wilson's clothes. Armed with this information the two detectives confronted Stuart Wilson in the interview room.

"I must have got the blood on my knuckles when I tried to revive her; the eyelash as well. I stroked her face with the back of my hand to gently wake her up," he claimed in a cocky fashion.

"Has your late wife been in an accident recently, like a car accident?" DCI Alex Crawford asked. He was looking up from reading the report he had in front of him.

"No, not that I remember but I know she was very clumsy, she was always falling and banging herself on furniture and the door frames," came the reply.

"How did you manage to get blood splatter on your clothes?" Stuart was asked.

"It must have been from when she breathed out her last breath!"

"We have statements from your neighbours stating you arrived home after you had already gone to work. Your footsteps could be heard ascending your stairway, you were reported to have been shouting out in anger. A loud argument could be heard on your landing about a blue estate car. They could hear your wife screaming and crying and asking you to stop. Then they heard something tumbling downstairs. They heard you screaming what sounded like, 'get up, get up' and then there was silence until the doorbell rang. What have you to say about that?"

The smile from Stuart Wilson's face had disappeared, his voice was no longer cocky as he spoke. "It's all lies, they made it up, they hate me and want me to get into trouble, that's what it is." He nodded his head as if to agree with what he had just told them.

Another question was fired at him: "How did the spots of blood get on the wall near the top of the stairs?"

"I dunno, probably when she was tripping up and banged her head against the wall before she fell downstairs, I wasn't there so I don't know what happened," Stuart replied with disdain.

The detectives terminated the interview, and Stuart was taken back to his custody cell to 'stew' for a while.

****

Two villagers in Blackendale were waiting for the bus at the bus shelter.

"Did you go to Amy's funeral, near Raystone?" asked a middle aged woman dressed in a summer dress and cardigan.

The younger woman was wearing jeans and a white top with a blue cardigan draped over her shoulders, she was clutching a shoulder bag in her arms. She spoke softly – "No, I didn't know her but I'll be going to Jane Hughes' funeral tomorrow, I believe her brother has arranged a big funeral. Villagers will be able to line the streets, to pay their respects, when the funeral cortege travels by to the church at about 11 am. A lot of people will be turning out, she was well known around these parts; she must have owned the pub for 20 odd years."

"It's such a shame, I didn't know Jane extremely well, I know she was always cheerful and helpful; she was a pillar of the community, we will all miss her," the middle aged woman replied.

The younger woman continued – "It will be Vera's funeral next. Poor dear, dying alone in that field in the dark, I shudder to think what she went through in her last moments. Her Jack Russell terrier will be with her now, he was put down because of his injuries and his old age, you know. The vet thought he would only pine to death for his constant companion, Vera. So, he thought it was best to put him down. I believe Vera will be buried with her beloved terrier in her coffin."

"I wondered what had happened to the poor dog Max, at least they will be together. I hope the police catch the killers soon, although they don't seem to have a clue. I heard they arrested a man; he was suspected of killing his wife – I wonder if he is responsible for these other killings as well?"

"Here's the bus, five minutes late as usual!" the younger woman exclaimed in annoyance.

****

Paul and Josie had nipped into town in their dinner hour to buy an engagement ring at the jeweller's shop. Paul had a limited budget but Josie didn't mind. She viewed the rings, bracelets, necklaces, and jewelled ornaments that were displayed under the glass counters. Josie was looking at the shocking prices as well as the beautiful engagement rings.

"Can I help you?" asked the young female assistant. She had a lot of makeup on her slender face and wore false eyelashes, she was dressed in a smart black suit and a white blouse. There wasn't a hair out of place on her elaborate hairdo. She had an air of aloofness about her.

"We are looking for an engagement ring," Paul replied nervously. He was conscious he smelt of oil and grease having come straight from work.

"There is a lovely selection over here, these are the most expensive ones but decrease in price towards the end of the display case," the young assistant remarked, looking at Paul in disgust.

Josie and Paul glanced at each other and walked to the cheaper end of the showcase.

"Hey, this one is similar to my dearest grandmother's engagement ring. I'll try it on, if it fits perfectly, I'll know it's the one for me." The assistant removed the tray from the display; her fingernails were manicured, covered in elaborate artistic nail designs. The assistant retrieved the selected ring with her long fingernails – it was a beautiful cluster diamond ring. It sparkled in the bright spotlights in the shop. Even the small jewels on the assistant's nails sparkled, making Josie feel conscious of her own poorly manicured, unvarnished nails.

"It's a perfect fit," Josie cried out as she slipped the ring on her slim finger. Paul grinned broadly; he loved to see her happy. He handed over his credit card to pay for the precious item. The ring was placed in a tiny box and handed over.

When Paul and Josie were sat in Paul's old light green saloon car, he clumsily retrieved the ring from the box with his large fingers. He slid the cluster diamond ring onto Josie's finger. Josie's eyes lit up and sparkled, she was extremely happy, they certainly had a wonderful future to look forward to. Paul felt the same, his life really had turned around at last. They tenderly kissed and hugged each other; they were both deeply in love.

****

The detectives resumed the series of interviews with Stuart Wilson.

"The spots of blood on the wall near to the stairs have been found to be Jackie's blood," DCI Alex Crawford told the uninterested Stuart.

"Well, it was bound to be hers, wouldn't it, when she tripped and fell! You haven't got anything on me," he replied with that familiar smirk on his face; he thought they were stupid.

"We have plenty on you!" the senior detective retorted. "You will go down for killing your wife. You have a history of abuse and violence on record which will help our case. Also, which is immensely important to this case, your neighbours heard what was going on, they are credible witnesses. There has been blood splatter found on your clothing too matching Jackie's DNA profile."

"As I said before, I could have got the blood splatter on my clothes when she breathed out her last breath," Stuart shouted.

"Forensics will be able to prove otherwise as she died instantly when her neck was broken in the fall," the lead detective adamantly retorted.

Stuart didn't think they had a concrete case against him; he knew he would be able to persuade a jury in his favour.

After the interview, the two detectives discussed the case and hoped they could link Jane Hughes' and Vera Williams' murders and maybe even Amy Lewis' murder to Stuart Wilson. They had all ordered vending machines from Stuart Wilson and he didn't have a solid alibi for any of them according to his wife, Jackie. Apart from Amy's murder where Stuart was at a meeting; however, the time of death could be wrong giving him an opportunity to kill her after his meeting. They knew Stuart Wilson would never confess to anything; it was, therefore, necessary for the detectives and their team to find the evidence against him. CCTV footage had been scrutinized again for the timeline between five and six pm; however, Stuart Wilson's car was only seen at between 5.47 and 6.03 pm. Stuart had later remembered he had visited his friend Colin after the meeting at the vending machine company, but Colin was out. So, Stuart had returned home; although there was no evidence to support this.

****

Blackendale village main street was lined with the villagers. Men took off their caps and bowed their heads in respect as the splendid, shiny horse-drawn funeral carriage with four jet black majestic horses, went by. The horses' black plumage attached to their black gleaming harness quivered in the warm breeze. The horses' coats shone in the bright sunshine, the horses' braided black manes looked smart and impressive. Clip, clop went their shodden hooves, they were painted in hoof oil, causing them to glint in the sunlight. Clip, clop, and the sound of the carriage wheels on the tarmac was all that could be heard as the crowds were silent. The driver wore black with a tall top hat, he was sat high up at the front of the carriage. A spray of white lilies adorned the polished, dark oak coffin inside the glass carriage. It was a spectacular site that had never been seen in the village before.

Jane Hughes' brother had made sure his beloved sister had a funeral fit for a Queen. The funeral cortege of mourners in black limousines followed at a distance behind the glass carriage on their way to the church. The church was packed full; many people had to stand at the back and outside listening to the service and joining in the hymns. Jane Hughes was later laid to rest in the adjoining graveyard near to her parents' graves. The two detectives had been present throughout the service, trying to see if they could spot the killer through any suspicious behaviour.

After the funeral, the wake was held in the village hall for the immediate family and close friends. The atmosphere was more relaxed – there was a splendid buffet laid out on tables, the room was filled with the hum of voices. The mourners tried not to talk about the awful murders plaguing their peaceful rural communities.

New Information

Paul and Josie had been busy contacting a local estate agent to arrange for Josie's house to be advertised on the property market. Photographs had been taken of the main rooms, the back garden, and the view of the front of the house. The couple were also making arrangements with a registry office for their wedding in the town. They were both thrilled about the upcoming wedding and were compiling lists of close relatives ready to invite them to their marriage ceremony.

They were visiting Amy's garden every day before work or after work. There was less work to do there now, as most of the vegetables and soft fruit had been picked. The hens still had to be fed and watered and their eggs collected. Thankfully, the hens were not bothered by foxes. Paul and Josie were looking forward to harvesting the apples and pears later in the autumn and there were still the winter vegetables – some cabbages, brussels sprouts, and the leeks to harvest.

"I've emailed everyone I know to tell them we are to be married and that you have inherited Amy's house, where we are going to live as husband and wife. I can't wait! They are all so excited for us, I've even put it about on my social media!" Josie exclaimed, shrieking with enthusiasm.

Paul grinned broadly, he loved to see her wildly happy. He knew he had found his soul mate; they were perfect for each other.

****

At the police station, the detectives were discussing the latest interviews from the party goers, where Stuart Wilson and his wife, Jackie, had attended a drunken party. Although the guests had all informed the police in the initial interviews that Stuart was there throughout the evening and into the late hours, there were doubts now in some of the guests' minds. They hadn't seen Stuart all the time as the party was in several rooms in the house and outside around the pool area. They were beginning to wonder if he had slipped out to kill Vera Williams and injure her dog; it was possible.

Other than doubt, the detectives still didn't have any solid evidence. It was extremely frustrating for them. At least they had Stuart Wilson in custody under suspicion for the murder of his wife, Jackie. There had been no more murders in the area since his arrest. Was this a coincidence or had the killer moved on? Was the killer in a hospital or in custody elsewhere at another police station? They wished they knew.

"Don't forget, seven pm sharp tonight, you know my wife likes everyone to be punctual," Alex told Sam.

"We'll be there, Annette and I are looking forward to it," Sam replied with his usual grin and chuckle.

The party was inside, in the large lounge, as the nights were quite cool and dark. Soft music played in the background, there were a delicious finger buffet and plenty of wine and beer for the guests. Paul entered casually dressed, with his girlfriend, who was dressed in a light coloured long sleeved dress. Jauntily, arm in arm, they approached a smiling Alex.

"Glad to see you both, I'll get some drinks for you." Alex turned to the homemade bar and selected some glasses, beer, and wine.

The room was full of guests; some new ones that they hadn't met before, along with the usual crowd of friends. Sam and Annette mingled amongst the crowd of people, still arm in arm, chatting politely. Sam felt more confident and relaxed with a partner by his side and was enjoying himself. Annette was an extravert and found it easy to make conversation with anyone, she had a way of making people laugh, they all enjoyed her easy manner.

Sam knew he had found his heart's desire; Annette was going to be his special bride one day, he hoped. He was looking forward to their weekend away in the Lake District, where they could relax more and become acquainted with each other a lot better.

****

The following day, neighbours at the other end of the lane from where Amy's cottage stood, arrived home. They had been on a long touring holiday in Scotland in their camper van. They liked to go away in mid-August to early September. They didn't listen to radio, television, or read newspapers while on holiday; it was a complete rest from all the day-to-day worries. So, they had no idea of the heinous crimes which had shocked the communities in their area.

Their telephone rang while they were unpacking.

"Hello, it's Jill, I noticed you'd arrived back from your holidays," her friend told her, who lived next door.

"Hi, Jill, we've had a wonderful time, seen lots of lovely scenery, we've done such a lot, I can't wait to return next year," replied Mandy excitedly.

"Have you heard about the murders?" Jill suddenly asked.

"Murders? What murders?" Mandy fearfully replied.

"It was poor Amy Lewis first, bludgeoned to death in her own greenhouse..."

"Oh no! Not Amy! ... Have the police caught her killer yet?" questioned Mandy, her mind racing with the disturbing news.

"No, and there's more! Jane Hughes from Blackendale

was murdered in her own pub on the day she was handing it over to the new owners. Her killer has not been caught either!" Jill explained.

"This is dreadful news; do the police think it is a serial killer?"

"I would think so, as Vera Williams was murdered late at night; on the footpath at Nick's lane here in Raystone; her dog was injured too. They have all had their funerals apart from Vera Williams," Jill replied with the harrowing news.

"This is a lot to take in, it's quite unbelievable, we've never had a murder around here before," Mandy remarked, very distressed.

"I thought you should know, no one is walking their dogs alone. Everyone is going out in groups, so don't you be walking your dog alone, it's not safe until the killer is caught. No one is going into their gardens alone either, everyone is terrified."

"No, I won't be walking my dog alone or going into the garden, I'm petrified now on hearing your news. Poor Amy, I knew her very well but not the other two women. When was Amy murdered?" Mandy inquired; her voice was emotionally choking up.

"The 18th August but she wasn't found until the following day, the same day Jane Hughes was murdered in her pub," came the reply.

"18th August, that's the day we set off for Scotland!" Mandy declared, astounded.

"What is it, dear?" asked Mandy's husband as he

entered the room; he could hear the distress in her voice.

"I'll go now, Jill, my Jim has just come in and wants to know the news. I'll come around later and we can catch up more."

Mandy told her husband, Jim, the dire news; he stood there with his mouth open. He was speechless for a moment, the murders had come as a terrible shock.

The excitement of the wonderful holiday and returning home had completely vanished, they felt extremely upset and numb. Amy was a dear friend and neighbour, they would miss her terribly, they were sad they had missed saying goodbye to her at her funeral.

Later that day Mandy popped around to Jill's house next door to hear more news. Her husband, Jim, had stood at the front door to make sure she arrived at her neighbour's house in safety.

"What time of day was poor Amy killed," asked Mandy, showing concern in her voice.

"In the afternoon sometime, it was a scorching hot day, do you remember?" came the reply.

Mandy thought back to the afternoon, her husband and she were packing the camper van on the driveway. She remembered a car driving by.

"That lodger, what's his name? ... Paul! He was driving past while we were packing up ready to leave!" exclaimed Mandy, remembering a few details.

Jill couldn't believe her ears. "Are you sure it was him; the police would have already interviewed him as he was close to Amy."

"Well, I could have been mistaken, it was only a fleeting glance, but I could have sworn it was his light green car, I've seen it many times on this lane when he was back and forwards from work when he lived with Amy as her lodger."

"Are you sure you have the right day?" Jill questioned, still not believing what she was hearing.

Mandy paused for a second. "I'm almost sure, surely he wouldn't kill the woman who thought the world of him? He adored her as well, it doesn't make sense."

"Well, as I said, the police will have interviewed Paul and he has not been arrested, so, he must have had a good explanation to tell them. My hubby caught Paul and his girlfriend, Josie, in Amy's garden a few days after Amy was murdered. Paul told my husband the police knew he was looking after the garden until things were sorted."

"Well, I must be wrong about the day; old age can do funny tricks to the mind," Mandy remarked. They both laughed and made a cup of tea and forgot about the murders for a while.

That night Mandy was tossing and turning in bed; she couldn't get the image of the light green car out of her head, she was convincing herself she had seen it on the day they were packing the camper van. She remembered distinctly carrying out the pillows and stepping into the camper van. On hearing the car, she had looked out of the camper van window and saw the back of the light green car.

The following morning at breakfast she spoke to her

husband, Jim, about the terrible night she had had. Jim had been quietly reading the newspaper at the other end of the table.

"I think you should inform the police – if Paul has a concrete alibi, it may have been someone else's car, the killer's car maybe, or it could be nothing, let them sort it out," he responded, closing up the newspaper and folding it in half.

"You're right, they should know. Jill told me – 'No arrests have been made for any of the three murders, so the killer is still out there'," Mandy explained, wide eyed with fear.

On the journey to the town, Mandy was having doubts about the car she had seen.

"I hope I'm not going to cause unnecessary trouble to that young man, Paul; it could have been someone else, I didn't see his face because the car had passed by."

Jim tried to reassure her. "The police will sort it out. You want the killer locked up, don't you?"

"Yes, of course, I do, it's just I'm nervous in case the finger is pointed at the wrong person," Mandy replied, her fears were building.

They had walked into the police station together for moral support. Until Mandy had told the police all that she knew, she wouldn't be able to get a good night's sleep, she wanted it off her troubled mind.

Mandy told her story to the attentive police officer behind the front counter. He typed in the information he heard, into his computer. He asked them both to take a seat; he knew how important this information was to the murder case, so he contacted the detective chief inspector dealing with the case.

They only waited a few minutes and were then asked to follow the lead detective, DCI Alex Crawford, into an office. Lots of questions followed; later in the conversation the detective wanted to establish a time.

"What time of day did you see the light green car?"

Mandy looked at Jim and continued with her answers. "After I'd seen the car go by, we had a drink, so it must have been around three pm or a little after." Her husband nodded in agreement.

"Did you see the driver of the car?" the detective asked.

Mandy quickly replied, "No, the car had gone by, by the time I looked up, I only saw the back of the car."

"Were there any stickers or anything on the back of the car or on the rear windshield to identify the car?" Mandy was asked.

Mandy thought for a moment. "I'm not sure, it was only a fleeting glance, I was used to seeing Paul's car going to and from work when he was lodging with Amy, so I assumed it was him visiting Amy which he does from time to time; I didn't even look at the registration number."

After the interview, the senior detective arranged to have the siting of the light green car near to Amy's property at the time of her murder relayed to the general public via local radio, television, newspapers, and on the local police news on the internet.

The DCI and his colleague, DI Johnson, decided to pay a visit to Paul's workplace at the garage and speak to his boss, to see if they could gain further information about their new suspect, Paul White. They parked on the forecourt and walked into the garage shop. Paul's boss was standing behind the counter, unpacking a box.

The two detectives introduced themselves, and the man asked them to follow him into the office in the back of the building.

"We would like to ask a few questions about Paul White, we believe he works here for you," one of the detectives began.

"Yes, Paul works here full time, is he in any kind of trouble?" asked Paul's boss in surprise.

"We are here to obtain any information which will help us eliminate Paul from our inquiries. Do you know if he has any money problems?" asked the detective chief Inspector, trying to establish a motive.

"I know he's always in debt! These younger ones put everything on their credit cards nowadays, instead of earning the money first, they have to have everything now. I know he likes a flutter on the horses, he's on one of these betting sites online. A waste of money if you ask me."

"How much does he earn here?" asked the senior detective. Paul's boss reached into a cupboard in his desk and brought out a book and turned the pages.

"£28,853 gross per year," he answered.

DI Johnson remarked, "It's not a bad wage, he is living with his girlfriend, so he should be able to manage on that." The two detectives had wondered if Paul's money problems were the reason why he had killed Amy; to steal money from her. The detectives left and headed towards Josie's Boutique shop in the town; to recheck Paul's alibi on the day in question.

Josie was surprised to see the detectives. She showed them into the small kitchen area at the back of the shop and closed the door. Her young shop assistant was left to manage the shop on her own.

"We have been given some information – a light green car was seen on the lane driving away from the direction of Amy's property on the afternoon of her murder. We want to go through Paul's and your alibi again, in detail, for the afternoon of 18th August."

Josie gasped in shock; she knew Paul had a light green car! Her mind began to whirl, surely, they weren't suspecting her future husband of murder!

"Tells us in detail what you and Paul were doing that afternoon."

Josie thought back to that scorching hot day.

"I had a severe migraine that afternoon, I took some medication and lay on top of my bed as it was so hot. Paul lay with me to comfort me; he was very worried about my condition, but I'd had many migraines before."

"What time did you go to lie down?" was the next question from the detective.

"It would be about two pm," Josie answered; she wasn't sure of the exact time.

"Did Paul leave you at any time?" asked DCI Crawford.

Josie suddenly realized he had!

"Yes, he did! I must have fallen into a deep sleep; when I woke up, Paul was gone." Josie was starting to feel anxious and upset. "I got up and looked out of the window, his car was still in the driveway though."

"How long were you asleep?" Josie was asked.

"I don't know, you lose track of time when you have a migraine, about 1-2 hours, I suppose" Josie answered, feeling like she was destroying Paul's alibi.

"Where was Paul?" The stream of questions were swiftly asked, one by one from the inquisitive detectives.

"I found him in the back garden; he had stripped down to his boxer shorts and was dripping wet," Josie responded. She was becoming very scared at the realization of the possibility that her husband-to-be could be a suspected killer!

The two detectives glanced at each other. "Did you see his discarded clothes in the garden at all?"

"No, I didn't. I asked why he was dripping wet, and he replied he had sprayed water from the hosepipe over himself to help him cool down," Josie informed them, becoming more distressed.

"Where were his clothes?" the DCI asked.

"He probably put them in the linen basket next to the washing machine. I'm not sure," came the uncertain reply.

Questions continued in a steady flow from the detectives. "Have you ever washed clothes with bloodstains on them?"

Josie gasped, "Definitely not, no."

"What was Paul doing in the garden?" DI Sam Johnson queried.

"He was digging over the borders," Josie replied, becoming even more doubtful about Paul. The detectives immediately became suspicious. Had Paul returned from the murder scene, stripped off, washed himself down, to remove all traces of blood, and was burying his blood stained clothing in the garden? He was always in debt – was he pestering Amy for money and she had refused to give him any? Had Amy turned away from Paul and he had struck her on the back of her head in a rage?

"Does he normally dig and attend to the garden?" asked the junior detective, trying to squeeze all the information out of her.

Josie was hardly thinking straight with the shock of what was transpiring. "Sometimes," she replied, "his job is mainly mowing the lawns."

"We wish to accompany you to your house and search the garden," DCI Crawford informed her. He was hoping she would agree, or else they would have to apply for a warrant and in the meantime, any evidence could be destroyed.

"Yes of course." Josie knew what they were thinking, they were placing a lot of doubt into her mind too. She urgently wanted to know the truth. She desperately hoped they wouldn't find anything to incriminate Paul. She was driven to the house in the detective's car. En route, the detectives asked her more questions.

"Is Paul fond of gambling do you know?" came an unexpected question out of the blue.

Josie was stunned. "Paul doesn't gamble as far as I know."

"How much does he earn?" the senior detective asked. He knew many who are addicted to gambling tell their partners they don't earn a great deal.

Josie thought for a second. "He told me he earns about £26,000."

Another question was quickly fired at her – "Does he have any other paid jobs?"

"No," Josie answered becoming nervous and scared as to where all this was leading.

They arrived at her small semi-detached house in the quiet avenue. Josie was thankful her neighbours would be at work, so they wouldn't witness the search and ask her and Paul questions about it. Josie led the detectives up the drive and along the path by the side of the house, to her small back garden.

"Which border was Paul digging when you found him in the garden?" asked DI Johnson.

"This one," Josie anxiously stated; she pointed to a border with roses planted in it.

"Have you a spade or fork we can use?" queried DCI Crawford.

"Yes, I have a spade in the shed." Josie walked to the shed and brought out a spade. The DI started to dig.

DCI Crawford apologized, "I'm sorry but we have to do this, we need to eliminate Paul from any suspicion."

"I understand, I can't believe Paul had anything to do with Amy's murder, he loved her... I want him to be cleared of all suspicion... We are getting married soon and moving to Amy's house, my house is already on the market!" Josie anxiously stated. Her heart was pounding in her chest, *please, please don't find anything*, she was praying to herself. Her life wouldn't be worth living without Paul. Her future was mapped out with Paul at her side; she couldn't believe all this was happening.

"I can't find anything here. Had all the borders been dug when you found him in the garden?" DI Johnson curiously asked.

"I'm not sure, I wasn't taking much notice, if he had dug all these borders, it's maybe why he was so hot and had to dowse himself down with the hose pipe," Josie declared, trying desperately to find an explanation why Paul was dripping wet. The detective continued to dig all the borders; his colleague was watching intently at every spade full of soil that was turned over to see if there was any sign of evidence. The junior detective found the digging hard work and had to partly unbutton his shirt. He was sweating profusely in the heat.

"We have found nothing here," DCI Crawford finally announced. "We will take you back to the shop."

Josie was tremendously relieved. It would have been incredible if Paul was accused of murder. She had never seen Paul, the person she knew as a loving and caring man, in a rage. She decided she wouldn't say anything to Paul about the police search, as she didn't want him to be upset. She knew how he had reacted to the suspicion of theft, at his place of work. The police had made her question about Paul's gambling though, *why would they have asked her that*? they must have known something she didn't know. She wanted to see Paul's bank accounts to see if he was a gambler but that would have to wait until he was out of the house.

That night, Josie felt exhausted from the upsetting events of the day.

Paul noticed she looked pale and subdued.

"Are you not so well?" asked Paul sympathetically. The black and white cat was rubbing up against his jeans as he spoke.

"I had a bad day at work, I feel so tired," Josie explained.

"I'll make the tea, you sit down and relax," Paul offered; smiling at her, he was genuinely concerned about her. Josie felt guilty that she had at times doubted his innocence that afternoon while she was being questioned by the detectives, Paul had always shown love and care towards her. She sat down on the sofa; the cat immediately made a beeline towards her and jumped on her lap, and curled up to go to sleep.

****

A few days later DCI Alex Crawford was pleased to receive information from a member of the general public. They had seen the police article asking anyone for information regarding a light green saloon car in the vicinity of Amy's property on the afternoon of her murder. The date and an approximation of the time, together with a telephone number to call was also given. A man who lived at the T junction at the end of the lane leading to Amy's property had seen a car with the same description. He saw it turning right, out of the lane and onto the main road.

"I remember it clearly," the man told the call handler at the police headquarters. "I was looking out of my lounge window and saw this idiot drive out onto the main road without looking for oncoming traffic, I took a good look at him to see who it was. He was a white male, clean shaven with short dark brown hair. I'd say he was in his 30s. I didn't know him."

"Was there anything else you noticed?" asked the police officer.

"Yes, there was a ruddy great horizontal scratch along the passenger side door, it looked as if he'd been careless before!"

"Are you sure this took place on 18th August?" quizzed the officer.

"Yes, definitely, it was my birthday! Me and the wife had returned home from a meal out at the pub, I wanted to get back to watch a programme on the telly at 3.30 pm," the officer was convincingly informed.

"So, what time did you actually see the light green car?" asked the officer, coaxing out more information from the caller.

"Oh, it would be about 3.15 - 3.25, I would think," came the reply.

"Did you see the registration number?" the police officer asked, as he was typing the information into his computer.

The caller had to think for a minute. "I hadn't my glasses on, so I couldn't see it all, but I know it ended with SMR."

The detective chief inspector was updated; he immediately knew it wasn't Paul White, who had a beard, and he knew Josie would be relieved when she found out he had been totally cleared from their investigations. The detective was desperate to know who this suspected killer was and was he connected to the two other murders?

An alert went out immediately with the information to all police officers in the area. Later that day, a police officer going home after his shift had pulled into a petrol station to fill up his car. While he was paying for it in the shop; he noticed a light green saloon car drive in to the garage area and park up in front of the shop. He was drawn to the long horizontal scratch on the passenger side door of the car. A man with the same description given had got out of his car and entered the shop.

The officer casually walked out of the shop and glanced at the registration number; the last three letters were SMR. He contacted base with the full registration number and details, and the name and address of the suspect were quickly obtained.

Amy's Killer

Josie received a phone call at the shop the following day. DCI Alex Crawford kindly told her that Paul was no longer a suspect in their investigations. He didn't want her to worry or call off the wedding. He politely apologized again for the inconvenience caused regarding the search, to check out her garden for evidence, and the many questions that had to be asked. The detective was still feeling guilty about Jackie Wilson's death at the hands of her violent husband Stuart Wilson. He felt he should have done more to protect Jackie. He didn't want Josie to change her life because of the investigations.

Josie was immensely relieved but still had the nagging doubt about Paul's gambling habit that the detectives had planted in her mind. During her dinner hour, she slipped home in her car. She found Paul's bank statements in a bank folder in his desk; she knew he didn't want to go paperless. She felt nervous looking at his private things. She had always trusted him before but she had to know – she didn't want to marry a compulsive gambler!

With the calculator on her mobile phone; she was able to work out that he earned more than he had told her, *he probably has had a raise in salary,* she pondered to herself. She sifted through his statements and realized he must have had a raise. She wondered why he hadn't told her, but subsequently, she realized it was around the time of Amy's murder, his mind would have been filled with the distressing news about Amy's cruel death, and she knew Paul had taken it extremely badly and was feeling low at that time.

She checked to see if there were any transactions of online betting sites on his statements, but she could only find three going back nearly two years ago. She felt extremely relieved but felt guilty she had checked up on him; even so, she was desperate to know the truth. She had seen films where men were very loving to their spouses but had a darker side; they would have a secret gambling or drinking habit or would be out murdering and raping women when they could.

Josie travelled back to work feeling relaxed and happy. Suddenly, she had to perform an emergency stop! A man had jumped out into the road in front of her car, he was frantically waving her down to stop. He was a white male in his 30s, with rolled up sleeves, his shirt was open to his waist. He was walking in a swaying motion, towards her car. Thoughts of the murderer on the loose entered her head.

Terrified, she immediately reversed the car at speed, she quickly turned in a roadway and drove away in the opposite direction. She travelled the longer route around to arrive at her shop. Her heart was still pounding when she arrived at work, she immediately rang the police to report the incident. She was told the man had been arrested, he was being drunk and disorderly, apparently, he was trying to stop traffic to obtain a lift home!

That night Josie relaxed in Paul's loving arms. What an emotional journey she had been through lately! She still felt guilty she had doubted Paul's innocence, she was now completely convinced he was the only one she desired to marry. She never mentioned to Paul anything about the police digging in her garden or them mentioning his gambling; that was all behind her now.

The following day, Paul and Josie arrived in the early morning at Amy's property; it had started to rain. So, they remained seated in the car hoping it would clear. They watched the rain droplets spot on the windscreen and drizzle down the glass.

"You know, with all the happenings about the murders and the excitement of our engagement, inheriting this property and arranging the wedding and everything, I've completely forgotten to tell you I've had a raise in salary at work!" Paul exclaimed, laughing out loud.

"That's wonderful news, you can now contribute more to our joint account!" Josie exclaimed, joining in the infectious laughter. Paul had finally told her, she was so relieved; she playfully tickled him under his arm. She knew he was very ticklish; he began to howl with laughter, Josie roared with laughter too, more from the reassurance that he didn't intend to keep any secrets from her.

The rain began to ease as they completed their jobs in the garden. Paul attended to the hens and collected five brown eggs. They both sat in the wooden shed for a rest.

"Amy showed me how to make soap one day," Paul remarked out of the blue. He had obviously been thinking about his time here with Amy.

Josie laughed. "Well, go on then, tell me how do you make soap?"

"It's easy, all you need is wood ash from the fire, it must be from hardwood though, animal fat and water! You make lye from the ashes and mix it with the fat to make soap, you can use any fragrance you like. Look, I'll show you."

Paul enthusiastically took a very large plastic funnel from the shelf in the stone outbuilding and placed it in a giant cast iron tripod, he put a filter in the funnel and filled the funnel with wood ash from a large metal container stood on the floor. It was where Amy stored the wood ash from the wood burning stove as there were many uses for it besides making soap. Paul placed an old glass bowl he had found in the shed under the funnel and began to pour water over the ashes; he let it drip into the bowl below.

"It's a bit like percolating coffee," he uttered with a laugh. While they waited for that process to complete, Paul built a small fire outside on the same site as Amy used to make her soap. He retrieved the house key from the ledge in the stone outbuilding and opened the back door to the house. He obtained a block of lard from the small fridge that stood on the unit top. Josie had followed him into the kitchen, amused and curious at this operation.

"I'm using lard but you can use bacon fat or render down fat from sheep and cattle which is called tallow," Paul explained. Josie was amused at his knowledge, although in the back of her mind she wondered if this was all a huge joke, he was playing on her!

Later, when the ashes had stopped percolating, he took the bowl of watery lye and poured it into a stainless steel pan. He placed the pan onto the stones surrounding the fire. He stirred the contents constantly with a wooden spoon and continued when the solution was boiling; the solution was becoming more concentrated as the water boiled off. As they waited for the process to complete, they chatted about all the other skills he had learned from Amy.

"Amy taught me how to filter water by all sorts of methods," Paul told Josie.

"Name one method for me," Josie inquisitively asked.

"Well, you can take a sock, put a layer of sand in it, followed by a layer of ground up charcoal and another layer of sand, and so on until the sock is full. Collect your water from the rain butt or from wherever and pour it into the sock. You catch the filtered water in a vessel below; you would have to boil it for 1-3 minutes depending on the elevation, for it to be safe to drink though."

"Where would you get charcoal from, if you were in a survival situation?" asked Josie trying to catch him out.

"Simple, you take it from your open fire, the wood that has smouldered but not burnt away or you make it!" he exclaimed.

"Come on, you can't make charcoal yourself!" Josie insisted.

"Yes, you can, all you need is a few dry sticks or logs. Make a tepee type structure with the sticks over finer sticks and dry leaves at its base. Cover the structure with packed mud or soil, leaving a hole; it's a way in to light the fire at the base. When the fire gets going, you close up the hole. The wood just smoulders and ends up becoming charcoal! I suppose an easier way would be to shove the sticks or logs into a metal can, if you have one, then put the can upside down in a larger can or metal barrel. Light a fire around the smaller can, in the larger vessel; in about three hours you would have charcoal!"

"Wow, you have learned a thing or two; from Amy!" Josie exclaimed in surprise. The lye was ready and was allowed to cool.

They had brought a picnic for their lunch, they sat on an old wooden garden bench to eat. They gazed on, admiring their work in the garden. The sky was clear blue, the birds were twitting in the trees, it was heaven to Paul and Josie. Paul returned to his soap making after lunch. He took the smallest egg he had collected and popped the egg into the lye solution.

"Amy used to say, 'if an egg or a potato floats in a lye solution, it'll make soap'."

Josie laughed – this was all very new to her; nonetheless, she found it fascinating.

Paul continued making the soap by adding the lard to the lye solution and boiled it down just as Amy had taught him.

"I'm only guessing at the amounts; Amy knew exactly how to do it."

"The whole process smells horrible!" Josie remarked.

"That's why you have to do it outside or it gets onto your lungs; I think it's the acid doing its chemical reactions." Paul continued stirring the mixture in the pan. The mixture, in time, began to whiten and thicken until it looked more like soap. Josie was captivated by the process.

"Now it has to be left to cure for a few days, I'll leave it in this oblong utensil with this cloth underneath. It's only a small sample but it will make a tiny bar of soap," Paul told her with a chuckle; he placed the utensil in the shed. It was late when they left this remarkable garden of memories and travelled home. Josie was feeling very happy and secure with her husband-to-be; she felt she loved him more deeply than ever before.

****

The police had arrested the man who had been seen in his light green saloon car at the petrol station. He had been followed by the police; they had made the arrest when he had returned home.

He had been taken to the police station for questioning. He refused to talk, other than giving his name – Gary Wood. He told them he didn't need a solicitor present as he had done nothing wrong. His fingerprints and DNA were not found on the database, confirming he hadn't committed a recorded offence in his past.

The two detectives decided to visit Flora to see if she knew anything about Gary Wood. Flora was surprised to see them again; she invited them into her flat.

"Do you know a man called Gary Wood?" DCI Alex Crawford began.

"No, that name doesn't ring any bells," replied Flora, deep in thought.

"Gary is a white male, clean shaven with short dark brown hair, he is 36 years old. He lives on Grange Road, not far from here," he informed Flora, trying to jog her memory.

"No, what has all this got to do with me?" Flora asked bewildered as to what was going on.

The DCI told her about the light green car seen in the vicinity at the time of Amy's murder; the car was registered to Gary Wood.

"You should have said, now I know – he's nothing to do with me though, I've never ever seen him; however,

I know he knows Amy," Flora replied, giving a funny little chuckle.

"How does he know Amy?" DCI Crawford asked, uplifted by this new information.

"Well, I'm 'letting the cat out of the bag' here! Amy told me not to breathe a word of it to anyone!" Flora chuckled again. "Amy's husband once had an affair, Gary was the result!" Flora swished away a wisp of grey hair on her face that was annoying her.

"Did he visit Amy regularly?" DI Johnson asked, leaning forward.

"No, he only visited her once I believe; Amy told me all about it. He went to see her after he heard his father had died. He asked if he could have some inheritance from his father."

"What did Amy say?" queried the DCI.

"She was flabbergasted, she told him his father had not left him anything in his will. She told him straight if he wanted an inheritance, he would have to contest the will; he would have to do it through the courts. Amy didn't want anything to do with him, she wasn't sure if he really was her husband's son or an impostor."

"Was his father aware he had fathered a child?" queried the detective.

"Ooh, yes. It nearly split their marriage. Amy eventually forgave her husband and he decided to have nothing to do with his son or lover in order to save his marriage. His lover didn't want anything to do with him either, she didn't want him interfering with her son's life; so, it made it easier for them both."

"Did he pay child maintenance?" the DI asked.

"Not that I know of," Flora murmured.

The detectives left happy they had determined a motive for the murder. Gary's car was examined for any evidence; his finances were also scrutinized. The officers realized Gary was heavily in debt, he was out of work and was way behind with the rent payments.

When Gary was interviewed again, he was told they knew about his visit to Amy's house. He readily confessed to that; he told them he had gone to ask Amy for some inheritance from his father.

The recorded interview continued.

"Your financial affairs show you are up to your eyes in debt, you are three months in arrears with your rent and have recently lost your job," announced the senior detective.

"So," Gary replied, sullenly.

"Your car was seen by several people, driving away from Amy's property around the time she was murdered."

Gary began to fidget; he wasn't aware he had been seen.

A police officer entered the room with a file and handed it over to DCI Crawford. "Here is the forensic analysis report on the car you requested," the officer stated, then left the room immediately. The strategic interruption was recorded, they hoped it would shock the suspect into talking.

The DCI silently read the report and looked at Gary over his spectacles. The detective showed no facial expressions of what was in the report, he passed the file to his colleague, DI Johnson. Gary was feeling nervous and wished he knew what was in the report. His hands were becoming sweaty and he couldn't stop fidgeting with nerves.

"According to the report a pair of brown driving gloves were found in the glove department of your car. Do they belong to you?"

"Yeah, I got them from my mum on my birthday," Gary replied, wondering where this was leading.

"They are a good pair of gloves; you must have been very proud to wear them," the lead detective added.

"Yeah, I always wear them when I'm driving," Gary Wood replied with a smile on his face.

"Your birthday was on 18th August. Were you wearing your brand new gloves on that day?" The detective knew this was the day of Amy's murder.

"Yeah, so what?" Gary retorted.

"The report here shows traces of blood were found on your driving gloves, they are at present being tested for DNA – will it be your blood or Amy's blood on your gloves?" The forensic analyst had swabbed the fine stitching on the gloves and found traces of blood around the stitching at the thumb.

Gary slumped in his chair; he knew it would be Amy's blood. He thought he had washed them thoroughly; he didn't want to throw away his good pair of driving gloves just because they had blood on them.

"Alright, alright, I did it, I murdered Amy." Gary cupped his hands around his head and cried; he was devastated he had been caught out, he thought he had got away with it; the sudden realization he would go down for murder was too much to handle.

"Tell us what happened that afternoon," asked DI Johnson.

"I parked on the back lane. I could see Amy in her greenhouse," Gary began to explain. He wiped away the tears running down his pale face with his bare arm and continued.

"I walked up the garden path, and she came to the door of the greenhouse, she knew who I was. I'd already told her I was her husband's love child the last time I was there. I asked her again for some inheritance. I told her my father had never given a penny towards my upbringing; my mum had struggled financially to raise me. I told Amy it was only fair now to give me what was rightfully mine." Gary took his handkerchief out of his jeans pocket and blew his nose.

He resumed his story in a low tone of voice.

"She again told me my father had not left anything in his will for me and if I wanted an inheritance, I would have to go through the proper legal channels and contest the will." His voice became louder as he grew angrier. "I was fuming, I had no money to do that, I was broke! And I told her so."

"So, what happened next?" asked the DCI.

"I pleaded and pleaded with her. She was quite adamant; the callous bitch didn't have any sympathy for me. She turned and walked away to continue to work at the bench in her greenhouse. She was ignoring me! I was outraged! How dare she turn her back on me, when I was so desperately pleading for money." Gary's voice grew louder as he became more enraged. "I picked up a heavy door stopper by the door where I was standing and lunged at her before she got to the bench, I hit the back of her head with all my might... She fell to the floor... that awful sound of her head hitting the stone slab, I'll never forget it... I realized I'd killed her..." Gary looked up as if he was pleading with the detectives, he didn't mean to kill her. "I was desperate for money, I honestly thought she would pity me and at least give me some cash, to tide me over." He shuffled his feet, he found it difficult confessing to such a heinous crime.

When the detectives heard him describe the murder weapon, they both glanced at each other; they knew they had the real killer. This information hadn't been released to the general public, so only the real murderer would know what murder weapon he had used. He was obviously not someone confessing to a murder he hadn't committed, which unfortunately had sometimes happened in the years the detectives had interviewed suspects.

With more pressure from the detectives, Gary continued his version of the events. "I thought I would see if her back door was open, I thought maybe she had money stashed in the house somewhere. I found some in a wallet and some coins on the top of a tallboy in her bedroom. I was relieved I'd found some money; in all, it was over fifty quid! It would see me through for a while."

"Where were you the following morning between five am and seven am?" DI Johnson asked in a harsh manner.

"I was in bed!" Gary exclaimed, realizing they were going to try and pin the murder at 'The Eaves' pub on him. He had read the newspapers; he knew all about the other murders. He had hoped that whoever went down for those murders would be accused of Amy's murder as well; so, he would be in the clear. He didn't think he would be accused of all three murders!

"Can anyone verify that you were in bed at that particular time?" the senior detective asked calmly.

"I live alone but my car was parked on the driveway so if anyone saw it, they would know I was nowhere near the pub at Blackendale, it's six miles away if that's what you are getting at." His tone of voice sounded angry at being questioned about a murder he had not committed. DI Johnson persisted on that line of questioning, asking if he had ever been to the pub? Did he know the landlady? Did he steal her handbag?

"No, no, no." Gary slammed his fist violently on the table, in frustration and anger.

The DI again aggressively asked where he had been on the night of Vera Williams' murder.

Gary flew into a rage, his face was red and his eyes bulged out of his eye sockets. Suddenly, he stood up, and his chair flew backwards across the room. He hammered the table with his fist, screaming, "I didn't kill her or that other woman, the only person, I've ever killed was Amy Lewis. So, don't you pin these other murders on me." He was scared at the way the interview was progressing.

DCI Crawford calmly told him, "Pick up your chair and sit down, Gary, we will be able to check your movements out."

Gary Wood was charged with Amy's murder after his interview and taken back to the custody cell. The detectives were relieved they had found Amy's killer at last; however, they still had another killer to find before he killed again and time was ticking by to Alex's retirement; the pressure was on.

"Hey, Sam, you were a bit rough on him in there, weren't you? We have a siting of a blue estate car at the time the pub murder took place – Gary has a light green saloon, it would be unlikely he did the murder."

"Well, at least we know he has a foul temper when riled," Sam replied with a smile.

The movement of Gary Wood's car was investigated on the CCTV footage obtained shortly after the pub murder. There was no sign of his car on any of the routes to and from the pub to his house that morning. His car was not seen going through the town on CCTV cameras on the night of Vera Williams murder either, so Gary was cleared for both of those murders.

****

That night, the killer of the other two women was sat in his lounge in his small flat. The monster in his mind was beginning to stir again, his 'better self' had contained the evil monster up until then; because his life had turned around for the better, but now, he felt angry, very angry indeed. The adrenalin had begun to flow as his anger grew; his breathing became heavy; his chest was slightly heaving. He'd been looking at his computer, watching the police in a foreign country unjustly lashing a young male to death during a huge protest march.

The evil voice was loud in his throbbing head, *kill, kill, kill*. He wanted to find revenge for the atrocious killing he had seen! It had brought back the painful memories of his brutal mistreatment from his aggressive and violent mother and the relentless taunting and abuse from the bullies at school. His 'other self' was out of control, he just needed to kill, anyone would do. He quickly dressed in his black clothing and walked unnoticed, out of his flat; it was late at night. He jumped into his car and slowly pulled out of the underground garage below the flats, so he wouldn't be heard.

Out on the road he felt a freedom sweep over him, *anyone was fair game to him now; even so, a copper would be a great prize,* his 'evil self' thought to himself. Driving along, he noticed a woman on her own; she was slowly walking on the pavement with her hands in her pockets.

The place was deserted. The tarty looking woman was wearing red high heeled shoes, a short black leather skirt that showed off her long bare tanned legs. She wore a light anorak pulled tight around her tiny waist by her hands in her pockets.

Excitement surged in the killer's whole body; his eyes were fixed on her, like a tiger on its prey, she was going to be his next kill!

The killer called out of his open car window, in a charming manner, "Want a lift, love?"

The young woman turned to see who it was. She had a lot of makeup plastered on her face and long false eyelashes flashing at him. Her light brown hair was tied up in a messy bun; she began to glare at him, spitting out her chewing gum on the pavement.

In a deriding manner, she called out in a loud voice, "Mi fella's with me, he's behind the wall, having a pee." As if to say, you're not good enough for me, I have a fella.

A tall, thickset, dark skinned male jumped over the wall and ran towards the killer's car. The killer quickly drove off; he wasn't going to involve himself in a confrontation with a man that size. The killer drove around for a while, but the streets were nearly deserted, and those people who were about were in groups. He was bitterly disappointed he couldn't find a lone victim; he would have to find one soon, his voracious appetite to kill again was overwhelming.

****

Paul and Josie arrived back at Amy's property straight after work. Josie changed into her old gardening clothes and wellies to complete her jobs around the garden. Paul still smelt of oil and grease from changing an engine in a car at work. He immediately attended to the hens. Later, Josie was curious as to how the soap had turned out after curing for a couple of days.

"Ooh, it looks like soap, shall we try it?" asked Josie grinning. Paul retrieved the key from the ledge in the stone outhouse and they both entered the kitchen with the small bar of soap tucked into Josie's hand. Josie handed the soap to Paul; he took the soap to wash his hands under the running tap.

"Gosh, it has cleaned your mucky hands!" Josie was amazed it was actually soap!

Paul laughed. "You didn't believe me, did you!"

Josie turned to laugh and kissed his bearded cheek as he wiped his hands on a towel. Paul swung around and wrapped his arms around her and gave her a passionate kiss on her moist lips. They held each other tight for a moment, dreaming of their upcoming wedding. It suddenly began to pour down; the rain was lashing at the kitchen windowpanes. They decided to pack up and go home.

When they arrived at their house there was a solicitor's letter waiting for Paul. The brown envelope was eagerly torn open; the typed letter was quickly read. He waved his arms in the air with jubilation, he was ecstatic.

"I can pick up the keys to Amy's house whenever it's

convenient," he shouted out; he was thrilled! "All the paperwork has been completed, I'm now the proud owner of 'Lane End Cottage'!"

"Congratulations! … You should rename it as 'Amy's cottage', in her honour," suggested Josie joining in the excitement.

"What a great idea, Josie. I will definitely do that." The cat had come through the cat flap in the kitchen door on hearing her owners arrive home. She ran through into the lounge to see what all the excitement was about; not amused she sat by the sofa, washing her front paws.

****

A few days later, a group of villagers was waiting at the bus stop in Raystone. The sun had started to shine, wispy white clouds were floating across a blue sky.

"I heard Paul White owns Amy's property now," stated an elderly woman, slipping on her silk headscarf.

"Wasn't he her lodger for a short time? Has he bought it then?" asked a younger woman, rummaging in her purse for some change for her bus fare.

Another woman with a small dog replied, "Flora told me yesterday, Amy and Paul had a special relationship, like mother and son. Amy had secretly told Flora a bit ago that she had decided to will the property to Paul as he had lost his parents; Amy wanted him to have the property for security. Just think, it would be like winning the lottery for him!"

"I wouldn't have minded someone giving me a property when I was younger," the soft spoken, elderly woman replied as she tied her headscarf.

"At least they've caught Amy's murderer now, it's that Gary Wood. He was always a loudmouth and used to swear something awful when he was at school. His mother couldn't handle him, she hadn't a strong enough character to match Gary's character. He should have had a father to keep him under control. They haven't charged him for the other two murders, so there is still a killer on the loose; we aren't safe yet. It could be anyone, the vicar, the solicitor, who knows? Everyone is under suspicion," the dog owner reminded them.

"Who is Gary's father? No one seemed to know; when I was in his class at school, we all thought his father must have died," the younger woman asked.

"I don't think anyone knows," the dog owner answered, picking up the small dog in her arms.

The elderly woman spoke up. "The pub murder, where poor Jane Hughes was killed, well, according to the newspaper, the police suspect it's someone with a blue estate car. Well, there is no one around here with a car like that." She retrieved her bus pass from her wallet and continued chatting. "I'm scared to death living on my own in that old house, it creaks and groans, it makes me on edge now, I'm always thinking the killer is in the house ready to strike."

"I still won't let my kids out to play, not until the killer is caught," replied the younger woman.

The elderly woman turned to see the bus coming around the corner. "Here comes the bus and on time too, it makes a change!"

The Arrest

Paul and Josie were able to start making a home for themselves, in Amy's cottage – now they officially owned the keys. They had decided which furniture was going to be sold and which pieces of furniture from their other house would be moved in. Curtains were swapped and favourite plants replanted in Amy's front garden. Josie had received an offer for her house, which she had accepted. Once they had moved to Amy's house, they were going to arrange to have a new kitchen installed and a few other minor alterations. It was drawing nearer to their wedding; the excitement was building.

****

The leaves were beginning to change colour into rusty browns, vibrant reds, and brilliant yellows; giving a dash of colour to the green landscape. The killer hadn't struck again; so, the villagers were becoming more complacent. Dog walkers felt reassured and started to walk out alone again, children began walking or biking home to and from school. Even walkers felt safe to hike alone.

Alex was becoming more concerned that the killer had got away scot-free. They still had no evidence other than the sighting of the blue estate car near the pub at the time of the Jane Hughes murder. None of the killer's DNA or prints had been found. Alex was going to retire in a couple of weeks, but it was unlikely he would retire in peace – he desperately needed to find the killer and put him behind bars, where he belonged.

"How was the holiday in the Lake District?" Alex asked his colleague, Sam, as he entered the office at the police station.

Sam beamed a smile. "Great and the weather was good too."

"We are having a meal at the Grand Hotel on Friday night at seven, would you and Annette like to join us, there will be a few others going who you know?"

"It sounds good, I'll ask Annette and see if she's free," Sam replied, grinning. They both sat at their desks; there was a mountain of paperwork to go through.

****

The following Saturday night, heavy breathing could be heard in the still silent air. His breath condensed on the cool air, forming a cloud of vapour. The killer was roaming about searching for a lone victim. He had tried several times on other nights but was unsuccessful. His frustration had reached a fever pitch; he would break into a house if necessary to kill; to satisfy his enormous appetite for murder and revenge – if he didn't find a hapless victim outside that night.

He walked along the footpaths in the fields hoping to find another dog walker. It was a full moon that night, its radiance lit up the patchwork of fields and the hedgerows. The hedges and trees threw a shadow over the perimeter of the fields where they overhung the boundaries.

The killer pulled his black hood over his head to shade his face; his gloved hand concealed his weapon of choice – a stone. He liked his victim to see him, he enjoyed sensing their fear, a fear he knew all too well growing up with an aggressive, violent mother. How he hated her; he would certainly have killed her by now if she hadn't died from excessive drink. Now his 'other self' was in total control – the monster inside him that had been manifested over the terrifying years of abuse from his mother, and the years of taunting and bullying at school from the other pupils – was now on the rampage, seeking power, manipulation, and revenge! His 'other self' desired to be the dominant one for a change, no one was ever going to hurt or bully him again! This monster inside him could never be contained, it was too strong. The monster wanted to dominate and control everyone; even kill as many victims as he could for revenge.

Suddenly he heard a noise, the adrenalin rushed into his veins, his senses sharpened, he was on high alert. He paused, listening intently, straining his ears to pick up any sound. He could hear the eerie screaming call of a red fox in the distance; the shrill hoarse scream sounded like someone was being tortured. There was a rustling noise in the hedge, perhaps it was a mouse or a bird. He continued to walk slowly, turning around occasionally to see if anyone was about.

The air felt damp and there was a smell of wood burning coming from the villagers' wood burning stoves. A horse in the adjacent field snorted through its nose, he could see the cloud of vapour in the cool air; the killer could hear the horse walking away from his direction.

Suddenly he saw a teenage girl walking in the field before him at some distance away, and quickly he sought out some cover in the shadows under a hedge. He watched her intently; she was humming to a tune, totally oblivious to her surroundings. *Her headphones she was wearing would prevent her from hearing any noise he would make,* he considered. Her long jet black, shiny hair flowed over her shoulders and shone in the moonlight. She was wearing faded blue jeans, ripped at the knees, and a light red and blue anorak. It was unzipped, showing her dark blue jumper underneath.

Unknown to him, the girl had climbed out of her bedroom window – she was on her way to secretly meet her boyfriend, whom her parents had forbidden her to see.

Her boyfriend would be parking up soon on the lane at the end of the footpath, further up the lane; it was their secret rendezvous.

The killer remained very still, his eyes had darkened with the adrenalin rush, his hands were sweaty in his black gloves, the excitement was surging to a crescendo. He could hear a barn owl in the distance, calling out with a long, eerie, shrill shriek, the girl never heard it with her headphones covering her ears.

His victim ambled towards him unaware a murderer was waiting to pounce. The killer suddenly stepped out, the girl was startled and gasped in shock at the surprising appearance of this tall dark menacing figure in front of her. Her mind was racing, *this must be the killer* she assumed with dread, her adrenalin surged, giving her the strength to flee. She ran faster than she had ever done in her life. Her silky, jet black hair flowed out behind her, away from her face as she ran like the wind.

The killer began to run after his young helpless victim, the chase was on! It was the most exhilarating part of the murder for him; he clasped the stone tightly in his right hand, he sprinted as fast as he could. The girl was terrified. He heard the same half whimpered scream coming from her mouth just like Vera Williams' last sound, he was enraptured in her fear. The girl desperately raced towards the stile at the other end of the field, but it seemed so far away. She was no match for the killer's long legs; he was gaining on her inch by inch at every stride!

He drew near. He lashed out with his hand that was gripping the stone – he missed! He tried again; she was zigzagging about to avoid him. It made him even more excited, the game of 'catch me if you can' was a tremendous thrill; he knew he would win in the end. It reminded him of when he was a young boy darting away from his cruel mother. He felt empowered now as he was no longer the terrified young child but the one who was in total control.

Finally, he managed to hit her on the back of the head, and she slumped to the ground in a crumpled heap. He stood over her, she was motionless and totally silent. His chest was heaving as he tried to catch his breath; he stood still, gloating at his latest kill. He was breathing heavily after the dramatic chase.

Suddenly a loud shot rang out! A large man came running towards him, shouting, "Stop that, you bastard, or I'll shoot."

The killer quickly tried to think of an escape route; he knew he was vulnerable in a wide open space with a shooter in such close proximity. The man was a farmer out shooting rabbits in the bright moonlit night; the killer knew the farmer was bound to be a good shot.

"Lie down on the grass with your hands behind your head," the farmer screamed, staying safely at a distance. The killer did what he was told. The farmer retrieved his own mobile phone from his anorak pocket; he didn't take the point of the gun away from the killer for a second.

"Margaret, it's me. Phone the police and ambulance

immediately, tell them to come to Long Gate field up Nick's Lane. There's a girl badly injured; I have the attacker at the end of my gun as well." His voice was hurried and emotional, he was extremely scared. He could hear his wife gasp in panic at the other end of the phone.

The killer had tried to move while the farmer was distracted with his phone call; until he heard the gun being cocked. The killer knew he wouldn't get away without being blasted with the shotgun – if he was shot in the leg, he wouldn't be able to escape anyway. He resigned himself to the fact he had finally been caught, his reign of brutal murders was over. The 'other self' dissipated leaving his 'better self' in full control and facing the consequences. The killer felt overwhelming remorse and gut-wrenching guilt at what he had done.

The girl was still lying motionless; she was bleeding from a gash to the back of her head. The farmer feared she may be dead; he daren't move towards her to check, in case the killer jumped him. He would have to wait; he prayed to himself; *please let her live*. All three of them remained silent.

The girl's boyfriend had arrived in his car at the arranged meeting place; it wasn't in view of the field. He didn't see the killer's blue estate car in the lay-by; he was parked further down the road. The boyfriend grew annoyed when his girlfriend didn't show up, he thought maybe she had 'chickened out'. When he heard the police and ambulance sirens in the distance, he thought he would hurry back home; it would look suspicious if the police caught him waiting there alone. He didn't want to be found there; the police would ask too many questions.

The farmer had waited for around 10 minutes for the police and ambulance to speedily arrive from the nearby town. It was the longest 10 minutes he had experienced in his life. He was relieved when he heard the sirens and saw the flashing lights rapidly approaching the field in the lane. Police officers and paramedics climbed the stile and ran across the field towards him. The paramedics quickly ran to the girl. The police officers ran to the dark figure lying on the grass. The killer's hands were forced behind his back and were handcuffed. He was lifted up by two burly police officers on either side of him and was walked away to the police car.

The paramedics were speedily attending to the girl.

"She's still alive but in a critical condition," one of them announced to the remaining police officers. The paramedics prepared her to be taken away on a stretcher while the murderer was taken to the police station to be questioned and charged. Another police officer was taking details from the farmer about the incident and asked for his name, address and telephone number; following this short interview, he was allowed to go home. They would contact him at a later date. The police found a blue estate car parked in the lane, suggesting this was the killer they had been searching for.

The farmer's wife was extremely emotional when she had received a call from her husband's mobile phone; he had made the call while he was trudging his way back home. She had waited a long time in a state of panic wondering if the killer had managed to overpower him and had killed her husband. When he finally arrived home, she flung her arms around him in an open display of emotion. She was so relieved he was safely back home.

"You are a hero now! You have caught the killer single handed and 'red handed' too!" she cried out, tears rolling down her face; she was immensely proud of her husband.

The farmer laughed. "I was only doing my duty, my fear is the young lassie might not pull through, it was the worst 10 minutes of my life. I longed to go to her to see if she was alive and OK, but if the killer jumped me, we would both have been finished off."

"At least the killer can't do it again. Was the girl anyone we know?" his wife quickly asked, drying her eyes.

"It was hard to tell who she was, she was lying face down, poor lass, but she did have long black hair," her husband told her, searching in his mind who the girl could be.

"I wonder if she's Kenny's lass?" his wife anxiously replied.

The concerned farmer responded – "We'll know soon enough."

The ambulance had rushed to the main hospital in the area. The girl was prepared for emergency surgery. She hadn't any identification on her and was still unconscious, so her parents, whoever they were, would have to wait.

At the girl's home, her mum had knocked on her daughter's bedroom door. When there was no reply, she opened the door and peered around the door; she saw Emma's room was empty. She rushed in and searched the room. She saw the window open and looked outside. Her anxiety was building, she suddenly realized Emma must have gone to meet her boyfriend. She was worried sick that her daughter was out there alone and the killer had still not been caught.

The mother frantically called to her husband, who searched the room, hoping to find some evidence of where she could have gone, but there was nothing. They rang around their daughter's friends; they were all shocked to hear Emma was missing; unfortunately, no one had seen her. The girl's father decided to call the police; he reported that his daughter, Emma, was missing.

It would be several hours before they heard the dreadful news about their daughter – a police officer had called at the house to inform them Emma was still alive but in an extremely critical condition in hospital.

At the police station, the killer had been going through the normal processing procedures. He was being co-operative; he readily gave his name and address. His fingerprints and DNA samples had also been taken. His clothes had been confiscated for forensic analysis, he was given temporary clothing to wear and was left to wait in the interview room.

DCI Alex Crawford had been informed that the killer

had finally been caught; he was given the killer's name and address. He immediately drove to the police station.

"I want a word with him alone, before the recorded interview," the DCI announced. Everyone understood his motive. The detective walked into the interview room and saw the tall killer sat in a chair by the table. The killer's eyes were downcast to the floor, he didn't even look up when the detective entered the room. Alex leaned over the other side of the table to where the killer was sat. He placed his hands on the table.

"Why! Why!" he shouted, leaning forward. "You had an excellent career and a good woman in your life," the detective screamed.

Sam spoke softly, "I've battled with this monster inside me since I was small, it's so evil now I can't contain it."

Alex had been shocked to the core when he had taken the phone call at home to inform him the killer had been caught and it was Sam, his DI! *Sam had shared his home life, his holidays and worked side by side with him! He obviously never knew the real Sam;* he had contemplated to himself.

"Why didn't you get help?" asked Alex, alarmed at his negligence.

"I thought I could control it; I've been controlling it since I was young. I came into the police force to stop violence and murder. Unfortunately, the more I saw of violence, torture, and murder in the world, the more this monster, this evil, grew inside me, it became more and more powerful; until I couldn't hold it back anymore."

Sam was clenching his fist in sheer frustration with how his life had turned out.

"What started it all?" Alex demanded to know.

"My mother was a drunkard, she was always aggressive and violent towards me, it was then I found comfort in a world of fantasy, dreaming up about monsters that would rip her to pieces. I absolutely hated her. It was the same when I was constantly taunted and bullied at school, the monster in my head would scream at me and tell me to kill. My 'better self' as I called it, would crush any ideas of violence that my 'other self' craved."

Alex had mixed emotions – on the one hand, he felt pity at the violence, pain, and mental anguish Sam had suffered while he was growing up. On the other hand, Alex loathed him for what he had done to innocent lives, that had left families destroyed and communities in a perpetual state of anxiety.

Sam continued – "When I was caught, I was relieved; I didn't want to go on killing; I wanted it all to stop. I was always full of remorse after the killings, I really detested myself for committing such atrocious crimes."

"Did you ever want to kill me?" asked Alex facing Sam, and looking at him square in the eye. Sam had been a colleague at work and a long time good friend. He wondered if he, himself, was ever in danger with Sam around him.

"No, I never had those feelings with you, my 'better self' was always in control," Sam meekly replied.

"What about Annette?" Alex demanded to know.

Sam screamed out with tears in his eyes, "No, no, I love her."

Alex could see the twisted emotional pain in his face.

Sam continued more subdued: "Probably in time my 'other self' could have turned on her too, I don't know, I really don't know. It's best I'm put away, then I can never kill again."

"Did you murder Jane Hughes in the pub and Vera Williams in that field?" Alex demanded to know; by this time he was fuming as he thought about these other savage killings.

"Yes, I murdered them both," Sam replied, full of repentance and regret. He lowered his eyes again – he couldn't bear to look his friend and colleague in the eye.

"Was it you who visited Ada's cottage in the lane?" Alex again demanded to know.

"Yes, it was me. My 'other self' was on the rampage and wanted to kill her too; thankfully she didn't open her door."

"Why did you steal from your victims?" Alex queried.

"I didn't steal anything from Vera Williams in the field, her pockets were empty apart from her keys. I stole from Jane Hughes to make it look like an opportunist, grabbing money where he could. I thought it would confuse the investigation. Later when I'd come to my senses, I was gutted at what I'd done, so, I gave the money away to charity."

Alex found it difficult to believe this was Sam, his detective, a colleague of his. Sam was a brutal killer! *How could he have known Sam all these years and not know there was something wrong with him?* Even though he owned a blue estate car and was six feet in height, clean shaven, and lived in the area being investigated – Sam had never been considered a suspect by Alex. Obviously being a detective, Sam knew how to dispose of evidence and not leave any trace of his barbaric deeds in his car or at the crime scenes.

"There's been a long gap in the killings – what triggered it this time?" Alex spoke angrily to him.

Sam looked at Alex, a broken man, and he slowly replied, "Annette broke off the relationship with me; she didn't want to commit to a long term relationship, as I did. I was devastated, I love her and was very happy to be around her. Back at home alone, my 'other self' took over again." Sam lowered his head in shame and remorse.

"Ah! I see now why you declined my invitation to dinner at the pub on Friday night, Annette had already broken off your relationship, so you didn't want to come alone," Alex uttered in an exasperating tone of voice.

"You're right, I couldn't have faced everyone on my own," Sam meekly replied.

Alex couldn't find words to describe how he felt, this killer was working side by side with him, investigating these murders while Sam knew all along, he had committed them himself! Alex was suffering disturbing dreams about the bloody crime scenes, these sightings would remain in his mind for the rest of his life. He realized that Sam was compartmentalizing these murders and his normal life – how else could he carry on so normally?

Sam had walked into the police station as a hero after alerting everyone about the red headed girl, Lizzie, who ran away from her parents. This was the other side to Sam, Alex pondered.

"If you had found Lizzie, did you intend to kill her too?" demanded the distraught detective.

"No, no, I was on my way to see Annette, I was happy. My 'better self' was fully in control!"

"Have you murdered anyone else we don't know about?" Alex asked abruptly.

Sam looked up; he saw the strain in Alex's face, and he answered meekly, "No, I would have told you if I had, my 'better self' is in control now and I'm relieved it's all over."

Alex remembered Sam's line of questioning in one of the interviews and asked, "When you were questioning Gary Wood so harshly over the murder of Amy Lewis and trying to imply, he had murdered the other two victims, were you in fact trying to pin your evil murders onto him?"

"Yes, I'm ashamed to admit it. I was scared, I knew all this was going to catch up to me eventually. I had Annette then, I wanted to make a real go of things and change my life around for the better," Sam replied, guilt ridden; he bowed his head in shame.

Alex realized though that Sam had killed Vera Williams after he had met Annette. He knew Sam wasn't being totally truthful. The thought of Sam enjoying every moment of the investigations of the murders and the power and manipulation, the fear and control he had over the communities, made Alex livid. Alex strode out of the interview room; he couldn't cope anymore, he felt sick to the stomach.

"He's all yours," he told the police officer who was standing outside the door.

Other senior detectives had taken over the case as Alex was too close to the killer. Alex knew Sam would go to prison for a long time and may never see the outside world again. It would be hard to rehabilitate a killer like that. The whole police force was in shock that the brutal killer was one of their own.

****

The villagers had arranged a special ceremony to recognize the farmer, Seth Walden, as a hero. He had saved the villagers from any more heinous murders by his brave act of making a citizen's arrest of this coldblooded killer who was plaguing their communities with his despicable evil. They awarded Seth Walden with a special plaque in memory of his selfless courageous behaviour. With the farmer's permission, the villagers decided to hang the plaque in the local pub, a tribute to the farmer's bravery, so everyone could see it.

The press and the television cameras were present at the official presentation of the plaque, held in the local pub.

The farmer didn't really like all the attention, but his wife was immensely proud of him and talked of nothing else.

Fortunately, Emma, the girl Seth had saved, had emerged from her coma; she had recovered quickly and was allowed to go home to be with her parents to convalesce. Emma's consultant was sure she would make a full recovery in time. She was lucky to be alive and was able to attend this special occasion in a wheelchair.

The farmer felt sorry that part of Emma's beautiful jet black hair had been shaved off for her emergency operation. The girl wore a wide brimmed hat to cover her shaven scalp and scars.

Alex attended the ceremony; he was there to represent the police force who had spent many hours trying to track down this abominable killer who had roamed their communities looking for victims. Alex needed to be there, he had one final act he must do to be able to live in peace. He gave a short speech, apologizing profusely to the communities that the killer, unfortunately, had turned out to be one of their own; a detective in their local police force. He praised Seth Walden for his fearlessness and courageous act of restraining the brutal murderer in order for the police to arrive on the scene and make an official arrest. He spoke of his admiration for Emma's strong determination to recover from her horrendous ordeal. All three were given a tremendous applause.

****

The following day, in Raystone, a group of people was stood gossiping in the village shop. The wind had started to blow outside, whipping up the fallen leaves and eventually bringing more rain.

"It's all in the newspapers, headlines are screaming out – 'Hailed as a Hero'; what a brave man Seth was to apprehend the killer like that!" exclaimed an excited middle-aged woman.

"I saw him on the telly last night! It's a good job he had his gun with him and he'd decided to go out shooting rabbits that particular night or the poor girl would've been finished off for certain," added another.

"I was absolutely shocked when it turned out to be the detective on the case actually doing these vile murders! You can't trust anyone in authority these days, he didn't look the type to be a monster," remarked the middle-aged woman.

"I know, it's terrible! I bet the senior detective working with him was shocked, I would have been! Fancy him not knowing!" replied the other woman. "Thank goodness we can all live in peace now and go about our normal lives."

"It's Vera Williams' funeral today?" interrupted a tall frail woman. "She's having a quiet family service in Leeds where her son, Jack, lives. Her dear Jack Russell terrier will be buried with her. Bless her, she never thought she would be a victim."

"It's a pity it's so far away, we would have all liked to have paid our respects to Vera and Max," replied the middle-aged woman.

****

Almost two weeks later, Alex walked into his office for the last time. He looked around at the four bare walls and his wooden desks and office chairs, and Sam's empty desk and chair. The computer standing on Alex's desk was a monument to the hours he had spent investigating cases. The old filing cabinet stood in the corner, a relic to the old fashioned way of storing information and photographic evidence when he had first joined the police force – index cards were used then. How advanced it had all become since he began working in the police force!

His long career as a detective had been extremely successful; he could enter retirement in peace knowing the recent killers would certainly be behind bars till the end of his days.

His other colleagues had arranged a surprise retirement party for him at his favourite pub – 'The Farmer's Arms'. It would take place when he had finished his final day's work. His devoted wife, Verona, would take him to this secret special occasion. She had not had an easy life being married to a detective and was looking forward to his retirement.

Alex and Verona arrived at the pub for a drink. It was there the surprise party was waiting. When Alex swung open the door, he was greeted by a crowd of people; they were enthusiastically clapping and cheering. He was extremely happy to see all his friends and relatives gathered there, and he laughed out loud. He had not laughed like that for a long time.

The one person he did miss was Sam, his fellow detective and friend for many years. Alex had been told that Sam had been charged with the two murders –Jane Hughes killed in the pub, Vera Williams found in the field, and the attempted murder of the girl, Emma, in another field. Sam had pleaded guilty to all accounts made against him, including theft.

Flora was a short distance away in her flat; she was excitedly thumbing through holiday brochures to arrange a cruise of a lifetime with the money she had inherited from Amy. It had been a long time since she had had a holiday.

The very same day Alex was retiring, Paul and Josie were on their way to be married at the registry office, in the afternoon – a few blocks away from the police station. Josie's proud father drove her to her wedding ceremony in his car. Josie was brimming over with happiness, she was finally going to marry Paul, the only man she had ever loved. When Josie and her father arrived at the registry office, her mother was waiting for her to help her out of the car. Josie was taken arm in arm by her delighted father and they walked the short distance across the room, to where Paul stood waiting for her.

Paul beamed her a smile. She could see his eyes twinkling, and she knew he was as happy as she was. Josie stood at the front of the room near a large oak table with Paul at her side. She looked radiant, her skin glowed with health and happiness. They both grinned at each other;

Paul mouthed 'I love you'; Josie's grin extended from ear to ear.

Their friends and family were seated behind them, there was a lot of excitement as they watched the proceedings. Josie wore a simple knee length wedding dress to complement her slim figure; Paul looked charming in his dark blue suit for this very special occasion. Josie couldn't believe she had ever doubted Paul's character, all he had shown her was true love and care. After the vows were made to each other, she heard the final words: "I now pronounce you husband and wife."

With all the love in her heart and an appealing smile, she looked into Paul's romantic, sparkling blue eyes. Paul bent down to lovingly kiss her on her alluring lips.

****

BV - #0084 - 020721 - C0 - 203/127/13 - PB - 9781914195556 - Gloss Lamination